"You wer
me today

"I didn't want you dropping from exhaustion at the day care center," Hudson said wryly, skirting the question.

Still, she kept her gaze on him. "So you'd do this for any of your employees?" She motioned to the meal and the house and he knew what she meant.

"No, I wouldn't. You're special, Bella."

Her pretty brows arched. "Usually when a man does something like this, he wants something in return."

He put down the wing he was about to eat. "Maybe I do. That kiss just didn't happen out of the blue. There's been something simmering since we met. Don't you agree?"

She looked flustered. "I don't know what you mean. I—"

"Bella, tell me the truth. If you can honestly say you don't feel any sparks between us, I'll drop the whole thing, take you home, not approach you again with anything in my mind other than a boss-and-employee relationship."

"That's what we should have," she reminded him.

"Maybe. Are you going to answer my question?"

MONTANA MAVERICKS: THE BABY BONANZA—
Meet Rust Creek Falls' newest bundles of joy!

Dear Reader,

If you've ever participated in a holiday pageant, you know how memorable they can be. I've been on both sides—as a teacher of second graders and as a parent. As a teacher, I watched the thrill and excitement of little ones practicing Christmas carols, dressing in their best finery, then singing their hearts out when they appeared on stage. As a parent, I knew the pride of watching my child become part of his class community and celebrating the holiday with enthusiasm and joy. There's a wonderful camaraderie among parents in the audience who are united in applauding their children's performance.

Bella Stockton, my heroine in *The Maverick's Holiday Surprise*, manages a day care center. My hero, Hudson Jones, oversees her and the goings-on there. When they are enlisted to help with the holiday pageant, they develop the idea to decorate baby carriages and let the little ones wear reindeer antlers. What can be cuter!

I hope you enjoy this Montana Mavericks Special Edition that I wrote from my love of romance, holidays and kids.

Best,

Karen Rose Smith

The Maverick's Holiday Surprise

Karen Rose Smith

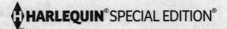
HARLEQUIN® SPECIAL EDITION®

Special thanks and acknowledgment are given
to Karen Rose Smith for her contribution to the
Montana Mavericks: The Baby Bonanza continuity.

Recycling programs
for this product may
not exist in your area.

ISBN-13: 978-0-373-65992-0

The Maverick's Holiday Surprise

Printed in U.S.A.

USA TODAY bestselling author **Karen Rose Smith**'s 87th novel was released in 2015. Her passion is caring for her four rescued cats, and her hobbies are gardening, cooking and photography. An only child, Karen delved into books at an early age. Even though she escaped into story worlds, she had many cousins around her on weekends. Families are a strong theme in her novels. Find out more about Karen at karenrosesmith.com.

Books by Karen Rose Smith

Harlequin Special Edition

Fortunes of Texas: All Fortune's Children

Fortune's Secret Husband

The Mommy Club

The Cowboy's Secret Baby
A Match Made by Baby
Wanted: A Real Family

Reunion Brides

Riley's Baby Boy
The CEO'S Unexpected Proposal
Once Upon a Groom
His Daughter...Their Child

Montana Mavericks: Rust Creek Cowboys

Marrying Dr. Maverick

The Baby Experts

Twins Under His Tree
The Texan's Happily-Ever-After
The Texas Billionaire's Baby

Montana Mavericks: The Texans Are Coming!

His Country Cinderella

Montana Mavericks: Thunder Canyon Cowboys

From Doctor...to Daddy

Visit the Author Profile page
at Harlequin.com for more titles.

To my dad,
who would have been 100 years old this year.
With his 35 mm camera, he gave me my love of
capturing memories with photography.
I miss you, Daddy.

Chapter One

Hudson Jones was used to getting his own way. But as he stood in the doorway of his office at the Just Us Kids Day Care Center, he had a feeling he wouldn't get his way this time. Bella Stockton had him stymied.

The day care manager was beautiful—tall and willowy with wispy short blond hair. He'd tried to flirt with her over the past month that he'd been here to see to the day-to-day running of the center. After all, a cowboy could get lonely underneath the big Montana sky. But unlike the other pretty women he'd flirted with over his thirty years, Bella didn't respond to him.

He studied her as she talked with a mother, one who'd apparently been involved in the parent-teacher conferences scheduled at Just Us Kids after normal business hours. Hudson recognized the expression on the parent's face. Over the last couple of months, he'd dealt with his share of upset parents. An outbreak of RSV—respiratory syncytial virus—had hit Just Us Kids, sending one of the children to the hospital, which had prompted her parents to file a lawsuit. The day care had been cleared, but the damage to its reputation had been done.

He moved a little closer to the main desk in the reception area where Bella sat.

Marla Tillotson was pointing her finger at Bella. "If I even see another child here with sniffles, I'm pulling Jimmy out and enrolling him in Country Kids." She turned on the heels of her red boots, gave Hudson a glare and headed for the door.

Although Hudson usually didn't commit too much time to any one place, he had taken this job more seriously than most. After all, it was an investment he didn't want to fail. He owned the property the day care sat on; his brother Walker owned the franchise. He'd let his brother talk him into staying for a while in Rust Creek Falls to oversee the staff and handle the PR that would put Just Us Kids back in the public's good graces. But, to be honest, mostly he stayed in town because he wanted to get to know Bella better.

As soon as he saw Bella's face, he didn't hesitate to step up to her desk. "It wasn't your fault," he said adamantly.

As day care manager, Bella ran a tight ship. She enforced policies about not signing in sick kids, incorporated stringent guidelines for disinfecting surfaces and educated the staff. But it seemed she couldn't put the whole awful experience of the lawsuit behind her.

Bella brushed her bangs aside and ducked her head for a moment. Then she raised burdened brown eyes to his. "I just can't help thinking that maybe I slipped up somehow. What if I wasn't vigilant enough before the outbreak? What—"

Hudson cut her off. "I'm going to say it again, and I'll say it a thousand times more if you need to hear it. You didn't do anything wrong," he assured her. "I read numerous blogs about day care and RSV when Walker asked me to take over here. RSV looks like a cold when it starts. Kids are contagious before they show symptoms. That's why it spreads like wildfire even with the best precautions. It's going to be *our* job—" he pointed to himself, and then he pointed to her "—to make sure an outbreak doesn't happen again."

Bella met his eyes intently. Suddenly the day care center seemed very quiet. Maybe it was just because he was so aware of her gaze on him. Was she aware of him? They could hear low voices in one of the classrooms beyond where tables were set up for the parent-teacher conferences. But other than that, the facility suddenly had a hushed atmosphere.

Hudson noted that Bella seemed to be gazing intently at him. That was okay because he was studying her pretty oval face. He missed seeing the dimples that appeared whenever she was with the kids. That's when she seemed the happiest. Her hair looked so soft and silky that he itched to run his fingers through it. But he knew he couldn't. This was the first time she'd even stopped and looked at him like this. Had she thought he was the enemy, that he'd pick apart everything she did? That wasn't his style.

He found himself leaning a little farther over the desk. He thought she was leaning a little closer to him, too.

All at once there was a *rap-rap-rap* on the door.

Sorry that they'd been interrupted, he nevertheless

excused himself and went to the door. When he opened it, the brisk November air entered, along with Bart Dunner, a teenager who was a runner for the Ace in the Hole. Hudson had ordered a mess of ribs from the bar for anyone who was still around when dinnertime came. He paid Bart, gave him a tip and thanked him. On the way to the break room, he glanced over at Bella. *Nothing ventured, nothing gained*, he told himself.

"Have you eaten?" he asked her.

"No, I haven't. I've been making out schedules and ordering supplies for the new year."

He motioned to the bag. "Come join me."

At first he thought she was going to refuse, but then to his surprise she said, "I skipped lunch. Supper might be a good idea."

As they washed their hands at the sink, Bella kept a few inches between them, even when she had to reach around him for a paper towel. Was she skittish around all men...or just him? Maybe she was just shy, he told himself. Maybe she was a virgin. After all, she was only twenty-three.

At the table, they each took one of the Styrofoam containers with ribs, crispy fries and green beans. "These ribs smell delicious," she said, and he didn't think she was just making conversation. But it was hard to tell.

As they ate, he tried to get her to talk. "You know, we've been working together for over a month, but I don't know much about you, except that you live with your brother and help with his triplets. I also know lots of people in town signed up to create a baby chain to care for the kids." Jamie Stockton had lost his wife, leaving him with the newborns to care for and a ranch to run. "That says something about Rust Creek Falls, don't you think?" If he could just get Bella talking, maybe she'd realize he was interested in her.

"That's the way Rust Creek Falls works," she responded. "Neighbors helping neighbors. And what you know about me is probably enough."

"Come on," he coaxed. "Tell me a little more. Did you grow up here?"

"Yes, I did. I was born here."

"Have you and your brother always been close?" he prompted.

"We have. I love my nephews and niece dearly." She took a forkful of green beans, then asked, "What about you? I know Walker is your brother."

"I have four brothers. But we aren't that close. Maybe because we've always had our own interests, or maybe because—" He stopped.

Bella studied him curiously. "What were you going to say?"

Hudson hesitated and decided he had to give to get. "Maybe because my parents never fostered closeness."

She gave him an odd look at that. "Our parents died in a car accident when I was twelve and Jamie was fifteen. We always had to rely on each other."

No wonder she didn't talk about her childhood. Losing parents had to be traumatic. "I'll bet you did rely on each other. Who took you in?"

"Our maternal grandparents took us in—the Stockton grandparents had both died. But Agnes and Matthew Baldwin didn't really want that responsibility."

"How can you know that, Bella? What starts that

way sometimes can turn into something else—a real family."

Looking troubled now, Bella shook her head. "When our grandmother died of a heart attack, I was fifteen. Jamie was eighteen. Our grandfather blamed us."

"You can't be serious." Hudson was outraged for her. How could her grandfather have even given that impression? But then he thought about his own parents and how cold his mother seemed.

"You don't know the situation," Bella said gently. "Jamie and I weren't the easiest kids to raise, and our grandfather was probably right."

Hudson was horrified that Bella actually believed that. She was one of the sweetest women he'd ever met. "You can't blame yourself for what fate hands out." But he could see she did.

Bella had torn apart her ribs at that point, and instead of trying to eat them with a fork as some women might, she nibbled the meat off the bone. Her fingers were sticky, and so were her lips. Hudson couldn't stop looking at her lips. She was in midchew when she realized he was staring. She stared back.

All eating stopped as they gazed at each other, and it was quite possible there was even a hum in the air. He wondered if she was just a little bit attracted to him.

But he never got to ask because one of the teachers popped her head into the break room.

"Got enough for me?" she asked.

That broke Hudson out of his trance. "Sure do, Sarah. Come on in and join us."

As the boss, he knew that was the right thing to do. But as a man, what he really wanted was to be alone with Bella. To find out more about her. To get to know her.

To kiss her.

Hudson let himself into the ranch house on the Lazy B, thinking that living in Rust Creek Falls for a while wasn't a chore. He tremendously liked where he was staying. He'd met Brooks Smith, the town's veterinarian, on one of his first trips to Rust Creek Falls. He knew the town vet could always recommend the best place to ride or rent out a horse. Brooks had done better than that. He'd suggested Hudson rent Clive Bickler's ranch.

Clive, an eccentric wealthy man who'd bought the property after the big flood several years ago, traveled a lot. Besides the main ranch house there was a smaller log home on the acreage where an older couple lived. They'd lost their ranch in the flood, and they lived on the Lazy B now and ran the place. Clive rented his home to high-end clients who appreciated his art collection and other niceties. Hudson, basically a trust fund cowboy, filled the bill. Living here was not only convenient but downright pleasant.

As he tapped in the code for the security alarm, he heard noise in the kitchen. That didn't bother him because he knew who was there—Greta Marsden. She wasn't only the wife of the foreman, but she also made sure Hudson had meals and treats to eat. Now she was loading a casserole into the refrigerator. The kitchen was all shiny stainless steel and high-end appliances. Not that Hudson cared because he didn't do much cooking.

Greta was in her fifties with silver hair that fluffed around her face. She had a wide smile and a kind disposition. She might have been a few pounds overweight, but she was fit in jeans and a plaid shirt. Her wool jacket hung over a nearby chair.

She glanced over her shoulder at him as she made room in the refrigerator for the casserole dish and smiled. "Do you need supper?"

"No, I had ribs. Not that they could stand up to anything you make."

She closed the refrigerator door, blushing a little. "You sure do know how to charm a woman, but save that for the ladies your age. I'm beyond it."

Hudson laughed. "You're not."

She waved his comment away. "When kids are grown, companionship and affection mean more than anything else. I'm relieved I don't need to look hot for anyone."

So that was what marriage developed into—companionship and affection. He wasn't sure his parents had that.

On the drive here, he'd thought about everything Bella had told him about her family. In fact he hadn't been able to get her story out of his head. He was still distracted by it now.

Greta bustled around the kitchen and pointed to a plastic container on the counter. "Oatmeal raisin cookies. These cold nights they'll go good with hot chocolate before you turn in."

"So you think I'm still a growing boy."

She laughed. "No, just a hardworking man with a big appetite."

Hudson wasn't sure about the hardworking part. He'd never really had to work too hard because his family was wealthy, so he was wealthy. He tended to take on jobs as he liked and then move on. His last project in Cody, Wyoming, had been about helping a friend start up a ranch—buying horses, choosing computer programs to manage the place efficiently. Over the years he'd managed ranches, wrangled cows and trained horses. This gig with Just Us Kids Day Care Center was something entirely new to him.

Greta looked around the kitchen and shook her head. "Edmond needed me to do bookwork today, so I didn't clean up here," she explained. "I'll be back to do that in the morning."

Hudson wasn't concerned about collecting a few dust bunnies. "No problem."

As he remembered Bella saying *Our grandfather blamed us when Grandma died*, he considered Greta's comments about marriage.

"Do you mind if I ask you something personal?"

Greta shrugged. "I suppose not."

"How would you feel if you suddenly had teenage grandchildren to raise? What if it happened overnight? What would you do?"

Greta didn't even hesitate. "Edmond and I would try our best to love them to bits. The people who come in and out of our lives are gifts."

When Hudson thought about Bella, he realized how she usually seemed sad unless she was around the kids. Had that been because of the way she'd been raised?

Apparently her grandparents hadn't considered her

and her brother as gifts. That had to color the way she looked at herself and the rest of her life.

Hudson nodded, suddenly a bit pleased with the evening. Though she hadn't revealed too much over their quick dinner, he had learned quite a bit about Ms. Bella Stockton.

When Hudson entered Just Us Kids the following morning, Bella was already there.

As he walked into the reception area, he tipped his Stetson and gave her a cheery good morning. Yet she simply murmured hello and hardly lifted her head. What was *that* about?

He wondered that same thing again when she wouldn't meet his gaze at a brief staff meeting before the children began arriving. He was sure something was wrong midmorning when Bella dropped time sheets on his desk without even looking at him.

She didn't act like a beautiful young woman of the millennia. It wasn't that she lacked self-confidence, because she didn't. With the staff, with the kids, with every aspect of organization, she was confident in her abilities. But not around him.

He had to get to the bottom of it.

Hudson had found he enjoyed being with the kids. It was odd, really. As an adult, he'd never been around children much. Several times a day he'd wander through the sections of children in different age groups. He knew many of the children by name, and they knew his name. He often stopped to help with an art project or just to converse with a curious four-year-old. They came up with the darnedest questions.

He pretty much stayed away from the babies, watching over them from afar. The teachers didn't seem to mind him wandering through. They often gave him a thumbs-up, and he praised them for the way they handled the kids. It wasn't an easy job, and he knew it. He'd handled two-year-old horses, and *that* task had seemed easier.

Throughout the day he often glanced at Bella and wondered why he was so interested in her. Her beauty, for sure, that pretty face, that pixie hairdo, that slender figure. There was something else, too, though—something that both unsettled and intrigued him.

He'd never been seriously involved with a woman. He'd never wanted to settle down because he'd seen the coldness in his parents' marriage. When he had dated, he'd seen that women wanted to tie him to one place. Moving from place to place gave his life the excitement romance couldn't. No woman had ever meant as much to him as not being tied down.

However, something about Bella Stockton made him want to get to know her a little better. He wanted to know why she'd gone all shy on him.

Late in the day, when only a few stragglers remained to be picked up, he had his chance.

He went to Bella's desk and asked, "Can I see you in my office?"

She looked up at him with startled eyes. But then she asked, "Do I need my tablet to take notes?"

He shook his head. "Not about this."

That brought a frown to her pretty face. But she followed him into his office, and this time he closed the door. He didn't claim to be a human resources expert.

Yes, he could spin a good story. However, this moment called for some honesty.

"I suspect you're not happy that I'm here to oversee Just Us Kids. But I want to reassure you I know you do a good job. My being here is just necessary in the wake of everything that happened."

"I know that," she murmured.

"Do you?" He looked at her directly, making eye contact, not letting her look away.

"It's not just *you*," she said. "It's *me*. I don't want to make a mistake. I don't want anything to jeopardize Just Us Kids."

"I understand that. Up until yesterday, I thought we got along just fine. At least we could have a simple conversation."

She didn't say anything to that.

He went on. "And yesterday, I thought we were finally getting to know each other a little better. I'm glad you told me a bit about your childhood."

"I shouldn't have," she quickly said.

"Why not?"

"Because Jamie and I don't like to talk about it. We don't like to think about it. Those were hard times for both of us, and we don't want anyone to feel sorry for us."

"And you think I feel sorry for you?"

"Possibly."

Hudson shook his head. "I'm sorry you and your brother went through that. I'm sorry your grandparents didn't treat you as the gifts you must have been." He found Greta's conclusion absolutely fit the situation.

At his words, Bella looked surprised.

They were standing near his desk, she at one corner and he at the other. But now he took a few steps closer to her. He could smell the light flowery perfume she wore. He could see the tiny line across her nose because it wrinkled there whenever she laughed or smiled. She didn't wear much makeup, but what she did wear was perfect—just a bit of lipstick and a little mascara from what he could tell. Simply looking at her caused heat to build inside him. He tried to throw a dash of cold water on it with logic, but it was hard to douse the kind of attraction he hadn't felt for a very long time.

However, he kept his voice even when he said, "It's a good thing when people who work together share bits of their personal life. They have a better understanding of what the other person has gone through. Do you know what I mean?"

She considered that. "I guess the way I grew up taught me that children should all be treated with respect and kindness and love."

"I can see that."

"And why do you treat them as if you're one of them?" she asked as if she really wanted to know.

"Because I never grew up." He was half joking and half serious.

Bella finally broke a smile. She looked him up and down, from his wavy brown hair, to the razor stubble on his jaw, to the open collar of his snap-button shirt, to his wide leather belt, jeans and boots. Then she said, "That's easy to believe when I see you with the kids. But it's hard to believe when I look at you as the supervisor of this place. You wear the role very well."

"It *is* a role, Bella, believe me. I'm only here until we're sure Just Us Kids has its reputation back, then I'll be off again somewhere else. That's what I do. That's what I mean about never growing up."

She shook her head as if she didn't understand. "But what's your purpose?"

"My purpose?"

"Before this job, what made you want to get up every morning and face a new day?"

"A new adventure. I went looking for it, whether it was gathering wild mustangs in Wyoming or managing the books of a friend's ranch during start-up. I have skills, and I have purpose, but that purpose isn't always the same. I find a purpose in the places I travel."

"With no commitment or responsibilities?"

"No commitment and no personal responsibilities. It's an easy, uncomplicated way to live."

"My life is full of complications," she responded with a little shrug. "I guess I wouldn't know what to do without them. But my commitment to Jamie and the triplets, and eventually finding my own future, gives me purpose each morning. It's a continuing purpose. Do you know what I mean? It's going to take me into the years to come. Yours seems like it could fall apart easily and leave you adrift."

Oh, he'd been adrift. He'd been adrift in between jobs, and he'd been adrift when he'd just enjoyed the scenery. But Bella seemed to think adrift was a bad thing. He didn't.

They gazed at each other for what seemed like minutes, even though it was only seconds. He found himself wanting to slide his fingers through her hair. He found himself wanting to step even closer. There was a sparkle in her eyes when she looked at him that made him believe that maybe she was attracted to him, too. But he was sort of her boss, and she already thought he was judging everything she did. How stupid would it be to get involved with her? Yet *he* set the rules here, didn't he? If he and Bella ever did really connect...

He suddenly cleared his throat. "I'd better open the door before anyone gets second thoughts about what's going on in here. I wouldn't want there to be any gossip about your reputation."

A shadow passed over her face, a definite shadow. Maybe he'd learned a little personal information about her, but not nearly enough. Just what was that shadow from?

But she wasn't going to confide in him any more than she already had. He could see that. She was already stepping away from his desk toward the door.

"Bella?"

She stopped.

"Are we okay?"

"We're fine," she said, raising up her chin a bit.

Fine. That was a wishy-washy word that didn't nearly begin to describe what he felt when he was in the same room with Bella Stockton. But he just nodded because he could see that's what she wanted him to do. He wasn't going to push anything...not yet.

Chapter Two

On Saturday afternoon, Bella was thankful for the baby chain that was helping her brother at Short Hills Ranch. This afternoon, Lindsay Dalton, one of the volunteers in Jamie's baby chain, had stopped by. She was taking over care of baby Jared while Jamie and Bella handled the others. By the stone fireplace in the family room, Bella was holding Henry and sitting in an old pine rocker she'd found at a flea market. His little eyes were almost shutting. Jamie had taken Katie upstairs to the nursery to try to calm her down. She was teething and couldn't be easily consoled today.

Lindsay sat on the sofa cooing softly to Jared. "If Henry starts crying again, he will, too," she whispered.

Lindsay was a pretty brunette and Bella could easily see why Walker, Hudson's brother, had fallen for her. Her own friendship with Lindsay had been strained by the lawsuit against Just Us Kids since Lindsay had been the lawyer suing Walker. But now Lindsay and Walker were engaged, and Walker was going to work mostly from Rust Creek Falls and travel when necessary. Lindsay and Bella were finding common ground again by helping Jamie.

"How goes everything at Just Us Kids?" Lindsay asked her, truly interested.

Bella continued to rock back and forth, watching Henry's fists curl. Holding a baby absolutely melted her heart, yet it made it hurt at the same time.

"Everything's going well," she told Lindsay. "At least it seems to be. We had a mother tell us that if she saw one baby with the sniffles, she'd pull her child and enroll him at Country Kids." Country Kids was their rival for clients.

"Sniffles and kids just go together," Lindsay said with a shake of her head. "Especially this time of year."

"One sniffle now and Hudson asks the parent to keep their child home. That's the way it has to be. I know that's a hardship on the parents, but we can't have another outbreak."

"I'm glad we can talk about this," Lindsay said. "I hated being on opposite sides of the fence."

Bella nodded. She'd missed Lindsay's friendship, too. "How are you and Walker?" she asked.

Lindsay's face broke into a wide smile. "We're wonderful. *He's* wonderful."

Then Lindsay asked, "How are you and Hudson getting along?"

"Fine," Bella responded airily. There must have been something in her voice, because Lindsay asked, "How fine?"

Bella felt her cheeks flush.

Lindsay said gently, "You know, don't you, that

Hudson has a reputation for being a love-'em-and-leave-'em cowboy."

"His reputation doesn't matter," Bella said. "He's my boss. That's it."

Still she remembered the way they'd sat together eating those sticky ribs, the way they'd stood close and she'd felt heat from Hudson and her own heat in return.

"You don't resent him overseeing you anymore?"

"I'm still not sure how I feel about that," Bella admitted. "But I'm not as resentful as I was at the beginning. I understand that both Hudson and Walker have to safeguard the business. I just didn't want someone judging every move I make."

"Is Hudson doing that?"

"Actually, no, he isn't. His managerial style is hands-off, unless he has to step in."

She thought about how Hudson had stepped in after a parent had dressed her down. She also thought about Walker's brief visits to the day care center and his sometimes condescending attitude to Hudson because he was the older brother.

"I wish Walker would tell Hudson he's doing a good job. After all, Hudson handled the PR for the whole problem and managed to keep most of our staff and our clients. But I get the idea that Walker doesn't understand what a huge achievement that is."

Lindsay rubbed her finger along Jared's chin, studying his baby face as if maybe she was contemplating having a child of her own someday.

"I hear what you're saying," Lindsay assured Bella. "But you know, brothers will be brothers. I get the feel-

ing that Walker and Hudson's relationship is complicated, so I think it's better if I stay out of it."

Bella admired Lindsay's honesty. "You're probably
right. I wouldn't want anyone interfering in my relationship with Jamie."

After the babies fell asleep, Bella and Lindsay took
them upstairs to their cribs in the nursery. Since Katie
was still fussing, Jamie carried her to his bedroom so
her restlessness and cries wouldn't wake the other two.

Downstairs once more, Bella and Lindsay cleaned
up the living room and den. There were always baby
things scattered everywhere, from bottles to diapers
to receiving blankets to toys. After Lindsay left, Bella
went to find Jamie, still in the recliner in his bedroom,
rocking Katie. In a pink onesie with a teddy bear embroidered on the front, she looked like a little angel.
He was looking down at her as if she *were* one.

"She's almost asleep," he told Bella. "But she's still
restless. I want to make sure she's really into a deep
nap before I put her down with the others."

"I can take her," Bella offered. "Why don't you go
riding? You need a break." He'd been up half the night
with Katie.

"I want to make sure this is merely teething and not
something else. She doesn't feel hot, but I want to be
certain she's not running a temperature."

Bella could hear the fatigue in Jamie's voice, and he
looked exhausted. He hadn't shaved today, and beard
stubble lined his chin. His blond hair fell over his brow
as if he'd run his hand through it many times. But as
he looked down at his daughter, his blue eyes were
filled with love.

Jamie was often overwhelmed; she could see it on his face and hear it in his voice. Yet he never gave up on the ranch, and he never stopped putting the babies first. He always gave them every ounce of love and caring in his heart, even if that meant he didn't have much of a life anymore.

She'd never regret quitting college and moving back in here with him. She loved helping him take care of the triplets. She loved being around the babies. But it was also painful. She so wanted to be a mother, but she knew she might never be able to have kids. Just how fair or right was that?

"What are you thinking about?" Jamie asked her. As a close sibling, he always could read her moods.

Her past played through her mind like a mocking newsreel. She could never forget about it, even though she tried. So she answered him truthfully.

"I'm thinking about how wild I was as a teenager."

"You were dealing with our parents' deaths."

"So were you, but you didn't jump off the deep end."

"Our grandparents didn't want us. I pretended I didn't care. I put my energy into sports. But you—" He shook his head. "You were younger. You needed Grandma's arms around you. You needed them to want you. They didn't. That's why we were separated from the others."

Bella sighed. Their sisters Dana and Liza had been younger, more adoptable, and had been sent to a group home for that purpose. Their brothers Luke, Daniel and Bailey had been over eighteen and had been turned out on their own.

"Don't you ever wonder where they all are?" Bella asked.

"Sure I do. But the fact remains that you and I haven't left Rust Creek Falls. Our siblings could find us if they wanted to. They obviously don't want to. Case closed."

Bella understood Jamie's attitude. After all, they'd been rejected by their grandparents. They didn't need sibling rejection on top of that.

"Sometimes I don't understand how you help me like you do," Jamie said, looking troubled.

"I'm your sister."

"Yes, but…"

She knew what he was getting at. They rarely talked about it, but today seemed like a day for stepping back into the past.

"I think she's finally asleep," he said, rising from the recliner and carrying Katie into the nursery. There he settled her into the crib and looked down on her with so much love Bella wanted to cry.

Then he turned back to her. "When you got pregnant, I didn't know what to do to help you. After you lost your baby and possibly the chance ever to have another one, I didn't know what to do then either. I don't know how Grandma and Gramps kept everything that happened to you a secret, but they did. Grandma died so soon after you lost your baby, and Gramps blamed you. And me. But keeping the secret about your miscarriage wasn't good for any of us…especially you.

You couldn't talk about what happened. You couldn't express your grief."

"Jamie," she warned weakly, not wanting to delve into any of those feelings.

"I feel like you're still grieving sometimes when you look at the triplets," he explained.

"You're wrong about that. I love being around Katie and Henry and Jared. They fill my life with happy times."

"I know sharing the triplets with you isn't the same as your having your own kids, but I want you to know I appreciate everything you do to help me and to take care of them. And even if you love being around them because they're your niece and nephews, don't you mind being around the babies and kids at the day care center? Isn't it just downright hard?"

"Actually, it's not," she assured him. "I think the day care center has been my saving grace. Your triplets and the kids there...they fill me with joy. I don't have time to be sad."

Jamie suddenly gave her a huge hug, and she leaned into him, grateful to have her brother. In that moment, she thought about having more, too—about having a man to love, a relationship, a life outside the day care center and Jamie's triplets. She thought about Hudson. She'd been attracted to him from the first moment she'd seen him. But she'd also realized what kind of man he was. He had a reputation, and she knew he wouldn't stay no matter what kind of electricity was flowing between them now. She shouldn't get involved...*couldn't* get involved. Besides, she had nothing to give somebody like Hudson. He had experienced the world.

And she was just a small-town girl who couldn't have kids.

Late Monday morning Hudson sat in his office much too aware of Bella at her desk in the reception area beyond. She really was an expert at handling the children. This morning he'd noticed the way she put her hand on a child's shoulder, or gave him a hug. Her smile when she was with the kids was absolutely radiant. Yes, it was safe to say there was a lot about the woman that intrigued him.

As if his thoughts had beckoned her, she stood and approached his office. He invited her inside.

"I set up a meeting for you with the holiday pageant director, Eileen Bennet, next Wednesday afternoon," she told him.

Every year the local elementary school put on a Christmas pageant, and this year they wanted the day care babies to get involved. "The pageant isn't that far off. I hope she doesn't have anything too complicated in mind."

"If she knows babies, she won't," Bella said with a smile. She filled him in on what she knew, then turned to go. She'd almost reached the door of his office when he asked, "What did you do before you managed the day care center?"

He'd heard the gossip that she'd quit college to help her brother, but he didn't know that for a fact.

"I was in college—my second year."

He must have looked puzzled because she added,

"I worked after I graduated from high school to save money for college."

"What did you do?"

"Mostly I waitressed. Lots of long shifts so I could sock the tips away. Four years of that, and I applied for and received a grant from a women's foundation. I enrolled at Montana State University."

"What was your major?"

"Business administration. I eventually wanted to focus on public affairs and learn strategies for helping small towns survive. Maybe that's a pipe dream, but if someone doesn't inject life into a place like Rust Creek Falls, it could become a ghost town. That was especially true after the flood."

"So your college courses gave you managerial skills that come into play here."

"I guess you could say that. I don't know when I'll be able to complete my degree. Working here will help me save the money to do it. But I plan to stick around Rust Creek Falls as long as Jamie needs me."

Bella's eyes sparkled with her dedication to her brother, as well as with the dreams that she still envisioned. More than anything, Hudson wanted to stand up and go over to her. He longed to brush her bangs across her forehead. Even more than that, he ached to tip her chin up, to bend his head, to put his lips on hers.

And that's why he stayed sitting. Yeah, he longed to kiss her, but they were in their workplace. Besides that, he wasn't looking for a long-term commitment, and Bella was the type of woman who deserved one.

This time when she moved to leave his office, he let her.

For the rest of the morning, Hudson felt unsettled. Finally he pushed away from his computer, stood and stretched. Truth be told, he wasn't used to sitting at a desk for most of the day. If he had to choose a job he liked best, it would be one training horses, cutting calves or walking through a field or pasture checking fence. He liked being a cowboy. Even now he rode whenever he could at the Lazy B, but it wasn't the same thing as being on a horse most of the day.

Leaving his office, he spotted Bella. Instead of at her desk, she was on a ladder at the bulletin board in the reception area. Instinctively, he crossed to her, fearful she was going to fall off.

As he stood a few feet from her, he could see that she was putting up photos of the babies who came to Just Us Kids. There had been an explosion of pregnancies after a wedding reception that most of the town had taken part in two summers ago. Rumor had it that old man Homer Gilmore had put something potent in the punch. The result: nine months later, nurseries had been full of babies. Many of those babies were enrolled at Just Us Kids.

He moved a little closer to study the photos, and Bella took notice of him.

"These pictures are good. Who took them?"

"I did," Bella said proudly.

She was still on the ladder, and he stood close to her, his shoulder at her waist. "You just didn't snap quick photos. These are well thought out, artistic even. Look at the eyes on this little guy. They absolutely sparkle." He pointed to another one. "And this expression is priceless. You have a real artist's eye and good timing.

Kids move and change minute to minute, and you've caught some of their best expressions."

She glanced down at him, and their gazes met. "Thank you," she murmured.

Clearing his throat, he said offhandedly, "You'd probably enjoy looking at the paintings at my ranch house."

Bella seemed to almost lose her balance. She toddled, and he put his arm around her to support her. They stood frozen, staring at each other, her face above his but not so far away. Why had she lost her balance? Had she thought he wanted her to come back to his ranch house for other reasons?

Maybe he did.

"You have to careful," he mumbled.

She nodded slowly. "Yes, I do." Then she pushed away from him and made her way down the ladder.

Once she was on the ground, he asked, "Do you have other photos you've taken? Not of babies?"

"I do. I carry my camera with me almost everywhere I go."

"Get it," he said impulsively. "I'd like to see them."

"Now?"

"You're due for a lunch break and so am I, right?"

Bella didn't know what to think of Hudson's suggestion. Did he really want to see her photos? Why? And just what had he meant by that comment about going to his ranch? Did he really want her to see the paintings? Or did he have something else in mind?

Did *she*?

She felt her cheeks beginning to flush. She didn't know what was wrong with her. For years now she

hadn't dated. She'd kept to herself. She'd been determined not to get into any more trouble, not to do something foolish or reckless. But in a way, her heart had
been frozen during those years. She'd rebelled as a
teenager, and that had gotten her into so much trouble.
No, she hadn't loved the father of her baby. Yes, she'd
been looking for love, and somehow she'd mistakenly
thought that sex could give her love. But she knew better than that now. She knew better about a lot of things.

But having Hudson's arm around her when she'd
almost fallen, catching the scent of his aftershave,
looking into his blue eyes, foolish and reckless and
impulsive had all seemed like good ideas.

No, no, no, she told herself firmly. *Hudson Jones is
nothing but trouble for you.*

Knowing all that, she still said, "My camera's in
my bag. I'll get it."

Going around her desk, she opened the bottom
drawer. Inside her hobo bag she found her point-and-
shoot camera. It wasn't anything special, but it worked
for her.

Taking the small white camera to Hudson, she
turned it on. Then she hit the button that brought up
the display and the photo review. "My SD card is almost full," she admitted, handing him the camera so
he could look for himself. She pointed to an arrow
button. "Just press that to go backward or forward."

He was silent for a long time as he seemed to
spend forever on each photo. When she glanced over
his arm, she saw he was studying the sequence she'd
taken on Short Hills Ranch. She'd shot the fall foliage
with horses in the background. She'd captured Jamie

astride a horse as well as a bay with a star on its forehead looking straight at the camera. There was a shot
inside the stable, too, where a yellow light cast a horse
in a golden glow.

As Hudson shuffled through one photo after another, she watched his expression. He had an expres-
sive face, not stoic like her grandfather's. She saw his
eyes widen with surprise when he glimpsed at a photo
he especially liked. She spied his mouth turn up at the
corners as he went through a sequence of the triplets
more than once. There was Katie with cereal all over
her face... Henry with his thumb in his mouth... Jared
crawling toward a favorite toy. She'd also caught Jamie
standing in a window at dusk, his profile in shadow.

Hudson suddenly lowered the camera. "Do you
know how good these are?"

She analyzed every crease on his face, the openness
in his eyes. Was he feeding her a line?

But his next words told her he wasn't. "I can see
you don't know how good you are. Did you ever think
about hiring out your services?"

"It's just a hobby."

"It's a hobby that could take you someplace. What
if I tell you I know someone who might like to hire
you to take photos?"

"Of what?" she asked suspiciously. After all, she'd
learned to be suspicious of men and their motives.

"Do you know Brooks Smith?"

The name sounded familiar, and all at once she
placed it. "He's a veterinarian. I've never met him.
His dad usually comes out to Short Hills when we
need a vet."

"Brooks and his dad have separate practices but cover for each other. His dad is cutting back his hours. Anyway, Brooks and his wife, Jazzy, run a horse rescue ranch out at the edge of town. The ranch is a passion with them, and they're going to have pamphlets printed about the facility. Jazzy mentioned she just hasn't had time to put it all together. Do you think you'd be interested in taking photos of the horses on the ranch?"

She was so busy now that she didn't know what to say. Between work and the triplets, she sometimes didn't have time to breathe. But the idea of taking photographs and making extra money was downright inviting.

"When would I have to do this?"

"Pretty soon, I guess. They mentioned handing out the pamphlets at their holiday open house."

"I don't have much spare time," she admitted.

"I know you don't, but this would probably only take a few hours."

"You don't know if Brooks and his wife would really want me."

"I can set up a meeting."

"Let me think about it. If Jamie has enough help, it would be a possibility."

Hudson motioned to the photos of the babies on the bulletin board. Then he pointed to her camera. "You have a gift, Bella. You see with your camera what most folks can't see with their eyes. You really should share that."

She thought about that, then asked, "Why? I mean, everyone sees what they want to see for the most part."

"But what if you can broaden someone's outlook? What if you could give them a positive spin instead of a negative one? What if you can make a difference?"

"We're talking about shooting a few photos." She couldn't keep the amusement from her voice because she thought maybe he was joking.

"No, not just a few shots. Each of your photos is a study of your subject that you've captured for eternity. That's not something to treat lightly."

She never expected something so deep to come out of Hudson. That just proved she didn't know him very well. And he certainly didn't know her.

"I'll check with Brooks and Jazzy," he said. "You think about it. I'm going to take a walk and get some lunch. Would you like some fresh air, too? You're welcome to join me."

She could hear the sound of children's laughter coming from one of the rooms. When she looked up at Hudson, she saw interest in his eyes. The children were safety. Hudson was danger.

As she had for the past few years, she chose safety. "I'd better stay here in case anybody needs me."

"You like to feel needed, don't you?"

"I do. It gives my life purpose."

He shrugged. "I've never had that kind of purpose. I'm not exactly sure what it feels like."

"Walker needed you here. Isn't that why you took over supervising Just Us Kids?"

"I never looked at it that way," he conceded. "I guess you're right." He motioned to the bulletin board. "It looks good. It will capture people's attention. Soon we'll have to decorate for the holidays."

"It's not even Thanksgiving yet."

"Not so far off," he reminded her as he moved toward the door. He opened it and looked back over his shoulder at her. "I won't be long. If anything comes up, you have my cell number."

She nodded. She did have his cell number. But she doubted she'd ever use it.

Chapter Three

As she approached Jamie's front porch, Bella couldn't stop thinking about Hudson and the way he'd studied her photos. He'd really seemed interested. She'd never thought of taking pictures for actual payment. That would be a breeze if it panned out because she loved photos and she loved horses, so she knew they'd be good. She hoped Hudson would really follow through with his offer.

As she opened the door to the ranch house, Bella heard commotion in the kitchen. Taking off her coat, she hung it in the closet and headed for the voices and the squeals.

She smiled when she saw the scene in front of her. Fallon O'Reilly was helping Jamie with the triplets by trying to feed Katie while he fed Henry and Jared. Bella felt warmth spread around her heart at the generosity of Fallon and others who were giving of their time so easily. However, the way Fallon looked at Jamie, Bella suspected there was more there than a friend helping a friend.

Fallon was a year older than Bella and came from

the kind of family that Jamie and she wished they'd had. She was a product of parents who had been married for decades and who loved their kids dearly. In turn, Fallon was great with kids. She should be; she worked at Country Kids Day Care.

When Fallon spotted her, she smiled. "As you can see, applesauce is on the menu. Katie is wearing it exceptionally well, don't you think?"

The baby had obviously waved her hands around with applesauce-covered fingers. There was even some on the little pink ribbon in her fine hair. She smiled when she thought how Jamie always dressed her in pink and tried to keep the ribbon in her hair so everybody would know she was a girl. He was such a good dad.

On the other side of the table, Henry and Jared had smeared it all over their mouths, on the high chair trays and even on Jared's nose.

"This looks like fun," Bella said with a laugh. "Can I join in?"

Jamie motioned to a chair on the other side of Henry. "Pull it up and have a go at this."

As Bella settled in, she said to Fallon, "How's everything at Country Kids?"

She brushed back her curly red hair. "Busy as usual. I had a four-year-old today who hit another child, so I had to call his parents to come pick him up. He was having a tantrum."

"How did the parents react?"

"Not well. But I explained that he couldn't disrupt the whole class just because he couldn't get his way. The mom admitted she and her husband are having some problems at home and that's why he's acting out. Her husband lost his job in Kalispell, and he's taken two part-time positions to try to make up for it. But they're having financial difficulties and arguing. All of that affects kids."

Bella exchanged a look with Jamie. Everything regarding home life affected kids. That's why she and Jamie were trying to give the triplets all the love and attention they could muster. With others joining in, the triplets should have a good start on life, even though they'd been born prematurely and had had to catch up. Even though they'd lost their mom.

"Fallon, I don't know if we say it often enough, but we're so grateful for your help," Bella said.

"I love helping." She turned her blue eyes on Jamie and then the triplets. "When these little ones follow me with their eyes, as they grab hold of my finger, or they eat their food instead of wear it, I feel like I've accomplished something important."

"I know what you mean," Bella agreed. "That's why I love working at the day care center, too. Babies are so easy to love." She thought about her background and Jamie's and added, "Unlike teenagers, who are angry and ungrateful sometimes."

"Our grandparents did their best," Jamie murmured.

Bella supposed that was true. People could do only what they knew how to do. But it seemed love should be easier to give than to withhold, and she'd always felt their grandparents had withheld their affection. She always surmised that they'd taken in her and Jamie out of guilt. Years before, they'd disowned their only daughter, Bella's mother Lauren, when she'd gotten pregnant out of wedlock, and Bella suspected they regretted that decision. When Bella had gotten pregnant, it had brought back for her grandparents all those unwanted memories and stress—stress that no doubt contributed to her grandma's death. At the end of the day, she had blamed herself for all of it. She'd ended up believing that she was a burden who should have never landed on her grandparents' doorstep.

Jamie's thoughts must have been following the same course because he said with regret, "I wish things were different with Gramps, but that's too much water under the bridge, isn't it?"

"I wish things were different around the holidays especially," Bella agreed.

Gramps still lived in the same house in town, and they never heard from him or saw him. She wished he could be part of their lives, but he'd disowned her after she'd gotten pregnant, even though she'd had a miscarriage. That hadn't made any difference to him. He'd been cold and mostly unspeaking until she moved out when she was eighteen. There was so much resentment there—resentment for his wife dying, resentment for the financial burden they'd caused, resentment that Bella had acted out when she was looking for love. No, there was no going back there. She just had to look forward.

"Family is complicated," Fallon agreed.

"Yours doesn't seem to be," Bella offered. "You're close to your brothers and sisters, and your parents would do anything for all of you."

"That's true, and my parents are great role models

for the marriage I'd like to have someday." Again her gaze fell on Jamie, but he was oblivious.

Bella knew her brother had always thought of Fallon as a kid sister. Would that change now that she was helping him with the triplets? Could that change when he was still grieving over Paula? Thank goodness for the babies and the others who were helping. Although Jamie didn't want to be beholden to anyone, the baby chain's presence in his life kept him from brooding, from being too solitary.

And then there were the babies. As she watched her brother wipe applesauce from Henry's little mouth, she knew the triplets had saved Jamie from grief that could have swallowed him up.

"As soon as we're done feeding them, we'll start supper," she said to Fallon. "Would you like to stay? I just plan to make tacos."

"I can chop tomatoes, lettuce and whatever else you want to put on them," she offered after she accepted the invitation. "That is if we get these rapscallions settled so we can have supper."

"We can take turns watching them and cooking, even if we have to eat in shifts. We'll manage it," Jamie insisted.

Her brother's gaze met hers. Yes, they were managing. But life was about more than managing, wasn't it?

She thought again about Hudson. All too easily she could picture his face and his mesmerizing blue eyes.

Bella stopped in the break room the following morning for a bottle of water to take to her desk. She was surprised to see Hudson there, opening a carton he'd set on a side table. Every time she looked at him, a little tremor started inside her and she wished she could will it away. It wasn't like she ogled calendars with pictures of buff firemen or handsomely suited *GQ* models for a little female thrill. But whenever she looked at Hudson, she felt a quiver of excitement.

She wasn't sure if it was caused by his long, jeans-clad legs—those jeans fit him oh so well—or the Western-cut shirt with its open collar where a few chest hairs peeked out. He was long-waisted and lean, and she could imagine exactly how he'd look seated on a horse. His brown leather boots made him seem even taller. Even without his tan Stetson, there was a rugged-Montana-guy feel to him that had to do with the lines of his face, the jut of his jaw, his dark brows. His thick hair waved a bit as it crossed his brow, and she found her fingers itched to ruffle it.

Crazy.

He smiled at her now as he flipped open the carton and took out...a blue teddy bear. Then he dipped his hand inside again and produced a green one and then a brown one.

She couldn't help but smile, too. "What are those?"

"Christmas presents for the young'uns. The day before Christmas they can each take one home."

"Did you do this?"

"Do you mean did I pick them out and order them? Yes, I did. It seemed like a great idea. There are three more boxes of them out in my truck. I'll stow them in the storeroom until Christmas Eve."

She approached him, telling herself she just had to pass by him to get to the refrigerator. When she did walk past him, she caught scent of his aftershave, something woodsy that made her think of pine forests.

She took a closer look at the bears. "They look child safe with their embroidered eyes and noses."

"That's what the online description said," he assured her. "I know how careful the teachers and parents are about those things. I learned that the first week I was here."

"You had a crash course in child rearing from the teachers."

"I did, along with the most tactful way to speak with parents. But it's darn tiring being politically correct all the time. It's much easier just to say what you think."

"You usually say what you think?"

"I try to. Less misunderstanding that way. I've had a few sharp lessons in life, teaching me to get to the bottom of people's motives really quick. Straight speaking does that."

She nodded, opened the small refrigerator and pulled a bottle of water from the shelf.

Now he moved a few steps closer to her. She wrapped her hand around the cold bottle of water, suddenly feeling hot. He unsettled her so, and she didn't know what to do about it.

"You were busy all morning, and I didn't want to interrupt you. I spoke with Jazzy Smith, and she'd like to see your photos."

Bella had considered the project but had doubts about becoming involved in it. "I don't know, Hudson. I don't even have a professional camera, and I don't know when I'd have the time."

Hudson gave her a long studying look. She had a

feeling he was debating whether to say something. But then he said it. "You're around babies and kids all day at the center, and you're around your brother and the triplets the rest of the time. Don't you think you deserve something of your own?"

She didn't know why his comments felt like criticism of her life. She'd had a whole ton of criticism from her grandmother and her grandfather. She didn't need any more from outside sources, making her second-guess what she was doing. Even her friends had been judgmental when she'd quit college to help Jamie. So before she thought better of it, she decided to say what *she* thought.

"You've no right to tell me how to live my life."

He didn't look shocked or even surprised, but rather he just gave her that same steady stare. "No, I don't have any right to tell you how to live your life. But maybe, just maybe, it wouldn't hurt for you to talk about it with someone." After closing the flap, he hefted the box of teddy bears into his arms and left the break room, heading for the storage closet.

See? she thought, mentally chastising herself. *Say what you think and it causes tension.* Yet on the other hand, her retort wasn't quite fair, not when he'd just seemed to be looking out for her. She sighed and went after him.

He was shuffling things around in the closet, apparently making room for the teddy bears.

Teddy bears. How many men would have thought of that? Let alone gone ahead and taken care of it.

He didn't look her way as she entered the closet, so she went right over to him and stood in his path.

"Hudson, I'm sorry. I shouldn't have responded like that. I guess you just hit a sore spot. That was my rebellious teenage side making an appearance."

He didn't seem angry. In fact, the look in his eyes made her breath hitch a little when he remarked, "I can't see you as a rebellious teenager." His lips twitched up a little in amusement.

If only she hadn't been, her life might be so much different now.

"You have no idea," she told him. As soon as she said that, she was afraid he'd ask questions. To forestall those, she said simply, "I'd like to meet Jazzy Smith. Did she have a particular time in mind?"

"Matter of fact, she said this evening would be good. If you're free."

Bella thought about it. "I'll have to call Jamie and make sure he has help for dinner."

"No problem. Just let me know. I can pick you up at your brother's. No reason for us to take two vehicles."

She considered riding in Hudson's truck, maybe finding a common interest that didn't include diapers and rattles.

"I'll call him now," she assured him and took her phone from her pocket, heading back to her desk. She could think better and breathe easier when she wasn't in Hudson's presence.

When Hudson picked up Bella a few hours later, Jamie was upstairs giving Henry a bath while Fallon finished feeding Katie and Jared downstairs. She called upstairs to her brother that she was leaving.

Bella explained to Hudson, "Giving a baby a bath can be tricky. Henry has his full attention."

"I'll meet him another time," Hudson assured her.

But Bella wasn't all that sure she wanted Jamie and Hudson to meet. Jamie was too intuitive, and her brother would sense her attraction to the man and zero in on it. She didn't want that happening. It was difficult enough to deal with her reaction to Hudson, let alone Jamie's reaction, too.

Hudson easily made conversation with Fallon. "I suppose you're getting ready for the holidays at Country Kids, too."

"We are. Artwork turkeys everywhere."

Hudson laughed.

"Fallon's such a good help with the triplets because she knows exactly what to do most of the time," Bella explained.

"Experience definitely helps when you cope with kids," Fallon agreed.

"I'm surprised you stop in here after work," Hudson noted. "Kids can be draining. I admire the way Bella works and then comes home and helps with the triplets."

"It's easy for me just to stop in on my way home," Fallon said. "And, like Bella, I love kids."

Katie banged her spoon on her high chair tray while Jared pushed round cereal pieces into his mouth.

"Are you sure you're okay for me to leave?" Bella asked.

"I'm fine. After Jamie's done with Henry, I'll take Katie up and give her a bath."

After goodbyes, Hudson walked Bella outside to

his truck. He went around to the passenger side and opened the door for her. "Need a leg up?"

Oh, no, he wasn't putting his hands around her waist and giving her a boost into the high truck. She could just imagine those long fingers and those big hands and the warmth she'd feel through her jacket...

Quickly she assured him, "I'm used to boosting myself up onto a horse. No problem with a truck."

Fortunately she was telling the truth. Clutching her purse and the photo album she was going to show Jazzy and Brooks, she hopped onto the running board and slid inside. Hudson closed the door for her, and she wondered if he was this chivalrous with every woman. Rumor had it he wasn't seeing anyone in town, but he could have a long-distance relationship with someone.

Once he was inside the truck and they were on their way, she felt she had to make conversation. Dusk had already fallen, and the inside of the cab seemed a little too intimate.

"Is the rescue ranch far?"

"Just about a mile from here."

"You said you're staying on a ranch."

"The Lazy B."

"That's a big spread," she said. "Any horses?"

"Oh, yes, some fine ones. Clive, the owner of the spread, has a good eye. He has two quarter horses, an Arabian, a Tennessee walker, a horse who pulls the buckboard and a Thoroughbred that was supposed to be racing but wasn't real successful at it. She's a beauty, though."

"Do you have a favorite?"

"I do. The Arabian, I have to admit it. I'm used to

quarter horses for cutting cattle and rodeo training. But that Arabian has eyes that can see into your soul. She seems to intuitively know what I want to do next, with a flick of the rein, with a slight pressure of a boot. Amazing, really."

"What's her name?"

"It's Breeze. Clive found her at the rescue ranch. Someone had abandoned her. After Jazzy worked her magic and got her back into shape, the mare actually trusts humans again. Clive named her Breeze because she runs like the wind. She knows her name now. At least, I think she does. She comes when I call her."

After a moment, he asked, "What's your horse's name?"

"How do you know I have a horse?"

"You said you liked to ride. So my guess is, Jamie has one just for you."

"Her name's Butterscotch. I ride her in the mornings when I can."

"I can almost picture her. Flying blond mane?"

"You got it."

Horses were an easy conversational gambit for them. Horse lovers were like any animal lovers. Talking about the beautiful creatures created a bond.

After a bit of silence, Bella decided to be a little bolder. "So what life did *you* leave when you dropped in here to take care of Just Us Kids?"

He glanced over at her, maybe to gauge how much she wanted to know. She could see his profile by the light of the dashboard glow. She imagined he could see her face only in shadow.

"I was helping a friend in Wyoming who'd bought a ranch. He needed help with the start-up."

"I imagine traveling place to place, you meet a lot of people."

"I do."

"Do you make friends easily?" From what she'd seen, he did. But she wanted to know what he'd say.

"I find something to like in most people. That allows for friendship, especially if I go back to a place more than once. It's really hard to keep up a friendship once you leave. I know the tech age is supposed to make it easier, but friendship still requires commitment."

He was right about that.

"Have you ever been committed to a woman?" she asked. She supposed that was one of the better ways to phrase it.

"No. Never anything serious," he answered with a shrug. "How about you?"

That was the problem with asking questions. The questionee thought he should return the favor. "Not lately," she said nonchalantly.

"Did you leave someone behind at college?"

"No. I really had my mind on my studies, so I didn't date."

He seemed to mull that over, and she wondered if he'd ask more about her past.

To her relief, he flipped on his turn signal and they veered down a lane to the ranch. "Brooks could move his practice out here, but he prefers to keep it in town."

Since darkness had fallen, Bella couldn't see much except for the floodlights on top of the barn that glowed over their surroundings. There were at least three barns and a house that looked like a typical ranch house but was much newer. It appeared big for two people, but maybe Brooks and Jazzy were planning on having a large family. Bella felt that stab of pain again that was never going to go away. It was one regret that haunted her.

Apparently divining her thoughts, Hudson explained, "Brooks and Jazzy plan to fill this house with kids. But they also have a first-floor suite set up for Brooks's dad when he's ready to move in with them one day."

"Then they must have a wonderful sense of family," Bella said, thinking about her absent brothers and sisters and whether she and Jamie would ever see them again.

When Jazzy opened her door to them, Bella admired her natural beauty right away. She was slim in skinny jeans and a tunic sweater. But her smile was wide as she welcomed them. She didn't hesitate to give Hudson a hug.

"It's good to see you again." She held out her hand to Bella. "It's nice to meet you."

"And you, too."

Bella handed the photo album to Jazzy. "I thought you might want to look at these. I don't have a professional portfolio, but I keep an album of the best ones."

"I can't wait to see them," Jazzy said. "Come into the living room. I fixed a few snacks. Brooks is out in the barn. He'll be in shortly."

Bella quickly glanced at the cheese tray, the biscuits that looked warm from the oven, jam and butter for those, and a fruit platter, too.

"You didn't have to go to all this trouble."

"It's no trouble. Brooks and I often don't eat till much later. I have something simmering in the slow cooker. I grab a snack with him when he gets home, and then we go out to the barns for a couple of hours. Rescue horses need a lot of kindness, soft talk and gentle touches. That takes time."

"Do you have help?" Bella asked.

"Some part-time help. There are also a group of kids from the high school who mount up service hours for working here. They learn from the horses, and the horses learn from them." She motioned to the food again. "Help yourself. I can't wait to take a look at these." She positioned the album on her lap and began turning pages. After a few pages, Jazzy glanced at Hudson. "You were right. She has a good eye—for scenery, for animals and for kids. That's a winning combination."

Just then Brooks emerged from the kitchen. "I came in the back way," he said, "so I could wash up. Hey there, Hudson."

Hudson introduced him to Bella.

"Look at these," Jazzy said.

"Before I even look, I can hear it in your voice. You like them," her husband guessed.

She just smiled at him and handed him the album. Bella lifted her camera, pressed a button and showed Jazzy photos she hadn't yet had printed. They were the same ones Hudson had seen of the triplets and of Jamie's ranch.

"Those are unedited," Bella told her. "I play with them a bit when I have time—cropping, adding a little light, studying them with black-and-white effects."

"I can see that with these," Brooks said, motioning to the album. "I think we should hire you."

Jazzy nodded and named a sum Bella could easily accept.

"I'd like a day with perfect weather," Bella said, and they all laughed. "Well, near perfect," she amended. "Do you mind if we do a last-minute shoot? I'll keep checking the weather day to day and, when I can get free, I'll text you to see if it suits you. Is that okay?"

"That's fine."

Now that business was taken care of, they snacked and talked, and Bella felt she really liked the couple. It was easy to see that they were deeply in love, as well as passionate about their work.

After she and Hudson left and they were in the truck, she said as much to him.

"You'd never believe they married for convenience's sake, would you?" Hudson asked.

"You're kidding."

"No. It had to do with Brooks's dad and him letting his son into the business. Then his father had health problems, and Brooks felt marriage was the only way to convince his dad to slow down."

"But they have more than a marriage of convenience."

"Oh, yes, they do. Jazzy and Brooks will be the first ones to tell you that they thought they were marrying for convenience, but they were really marrying for love."

Bella and Hudson didn't talk after that, and she wondered if they were both thinking about what he'd said. She couldn't remember much about her own parents' marriage, but she believed they'd been in love. She remembered them holding hands. She remembered them kissing when they thought their children weren't looking. But she'd never know that kind of love. Men wanted children, and she couldn't have them.

Back at the ranch, she'd thought she'd just hop out of Hudson's truck and that would be it. But no, he was being chivalrous again. He came around to her side and opened the door for her. He even took her hand to help her out. That was the first they'd touched all evening. His fingers seemed to burn hers. And when she was on the ground, she looked up at him, confused by all of it. They walked side by side to the front door, then just stood there gazing at each other.

"It *was* nice," he finally said, "sitting there with Jazzy and Brooks, talking like we're friends."

"Yes. Most of my friends are single women."

"They really liked your photos. This could be just the first of many assignments. Word gets around, you know."

"It would be fun to take photos to pay bills. I can also save some money for college."

"No splurging?"

She could hardly think straight looking into Hudson's eyes. "No splurging," she said softly.

He took a step closer to her, and Bella knew she should back away. But she didn't.

Hudson reached out and touched her cheek. Her face was cold from the winter night air, and his hand was large and warm. She could feel calluses on his fingers, and that was exciting. Everything about Hudson was exciting. When his hand went to the nape of her neck and he slid his fingers into her hair, she should have protested. She didn't. And when he bent his head, she knew exactly what he was going to do.

Chapter Four

If he'd thought this kiss was going to be something easy or quiet, Hudson had been dead wrong. Bella had a sweetness about her that revved up his male instincts and all his male needs. The hunger that welled inside him wasn't going to be satisfied with just a quick tasting.

Some essence of her made him want to get closer and know her in an intimate way. He wrapped his arm around her, maybe to steady them both.

He'd kissed a lot of women, and he'd wanted to demonstrate finesse with this kiss. But finesse floated out the window when his tongue breached Bella's lips. He swept her mouth with an intensity that disconcerted him. No, one brief kiss wasn't going to be enough. He felt intoxicated by their passion and confident in her response. She was tasting him, too, giving back passion as well as receiving it.

But then suddenly she wasn't. It was as if a switch had been flicked off. He felt her stiffen, and he knew exactly what was going to come between them. Rational thought. It had invaded her head before it had found its way to his.

Suddenly she was breaking away, her arms stiff at her sides. She was shaking her head, and he knew whatever she said wasn't going to be good.

Still, he was old enough and experienced enough and respectful of females enough, not to take what a woman didn't want to give. He tried to shut down the heavy beating of his pulse. With a deep breath, he willed his body to calm down, letting her escape his arms. He kept his hands by his sides even though he wanted to still touch her, even though he wanted to wrap her in another embrace.

"What's wrong?" he asked, surprised his voice had come out as even as it had. After all, that kiss had practically knocked his boots off.

"I can't do this," she said, shaking her head again. "I need my job. I can't get involved with you."

As if a bolt of lightning had made him see more clearly, Hudson suddenly realized that everything about Bella's life was so much more precarious than his. Although his parents had been distant emotionally, he'd had four brothers. Someone was always there. And besides his family, his father's wealth had been a life raft. His own trust fund had given him opportunities and saved him from embarrassing situations. When something didn't work out, he moved on to the next endeavor because he didn't have to count on a paycheck. Bella didn't have that luxury. She worried about her brother and her niece and nephews and about Jamie's financial situation. She worried about her own.

She was trying to save enough money to finish college, and Hudson knew how expensive that was these days.

The porch lamp softly glowed across her face. He saw her expression that said she already might have done something that would put her job in jeopardy. That was because she didn't know him. She didn't know what kind of man he was, and that he'd never punish a woman for backing away from him.

"Bella, it's all right. I understand."

"You're not mad because I wouldn't—" She stopped, seemingly embarrassed to go on.

"Nothing's going to interfere with your job, whether we kiss or whether we don't."

"It's too dangerous for me to even think about getting involved with you," she responded. "I can't risk one of the few jobs in Rust Creek Falls that pays decently. It isn't just you. It's Walker, too. He owns Just Us Kids. If anything happened between you and me, he could blame me."

This time Hudson took hold of her shoulders. He couldn't help touching her. "Stop, Bella. I do understand. No repercussions. I read the signals wrong."

At that she blinked, and then she sighed. "I can't let you think that. You didn't read the signals wrong. But I remembered my responsibilities. I remembered who I am and who you are. We come from different worlds, Hudson."

"It was just a kiss, Bella."

After she studied him for a few seconds, she nodded. "Okay, it was just a kiss. I have to go inside. I'm sure Jamie heard the truck, and he'll wonder why I'm still out here."

Hudson dropped his hands away from her because he knew she was going to run. He couldn't blame her, for all the reasons she'd mentioned. Yet when she turned the knob on the door, when she glanced at him over her shoulder, he got the feeling she didn't want to go inside at all.

She said good-night, and so did he. But as he went to his truck, he remembered everything about their kiss, and he wondered if she was doing the same.

Hudson understood Bella's avoidance of him—he really did. That didn't mean he was less attracted to her. Nor did that change the electricity that zapped between them whenever they had to deal with each other. First, when he stole glances at her and saw the dark circles under her eyes, he wondered if the tension between them was causing it. But as the week passed, he didn't think that was it at all. Bella worked all day, and he'd heard her tell one of the teachers that two of the triplets had kept her and Jamie up for the past few nights teething. He might not understand what that was all about, but he did understand sleep deprivation. She wasn't smiling at everyone the way she usually did. The next day at lunchtime, he walked into the break room and found her arms crossed on the table with her head down on them. She was asleep.

She didn't stir as he approached her and stood at the table looking down at her. Her eyes were closed, the lashes fanning her cheeks. Her hair wisped along her face, looking as silky and soft as always. He couldn't let her try to function like this.

Placing his hand on her shoulder, he said gently, "Bella?"

Her eyes fluttered open immediately. She turned her head, spotted him and sat up straight. "Sorry," she murmured. "I was just—"

"You were catching forty winks."

"It's my lunch break," she said, almost defensively, as if he'd caught her doing something terribly wrong.

"I understand that, and if we had a cot in here where you could take a nap like the kids do, you'd be fine. But you're not getting enough sleep, are you?"

"Katie and Henry have new teeth coming in. They're miserable. At first Jamie and I took turns, but it's hard to handle two at once. So we've both been up rocking and walking them."

"You have to get some sleep. Take the afternoon off, go home and go to bed."

"I can't do that."

He suddenly realized she meant *can't* in a couple of different ways. "You mean because you're needed here?"

"Yes, I am."

"I can take over for the afternoon. It's Friday. Things have slowed down for the week."

But Bella wasn't convinced, and then he realized what the other problem might be. "You won't be able to rest if you go back to Jamie's, will you? I should have realized that. Let me take you to my house so you can get a few hours of sleep without disruption."

Bella's eyes went wide, and he knew exactly what she was thinking. "I'll let you in, turn off the alarm and then I'll come back here. You can sleep on the sofa or a bed or wherever you want. The place will be yours for a few hours."

"Hudson, it's your home. I can't just barge in and take over."

"Sure you can. Tell me, how much time have you had absolutely alone since you moved in with Jamie?"

The question obviously didn't need much thinking about. She answered immediately. "I'm alone in my drives to and from work, and if I manage to go for a ride to exercise the horses."

"And how often do you do that?"

"I haven't for a couple of weeks," she admitted.

"Exactly. You have noise and kids around you almost twenty-four hours a day. Give yourself a break, Bella. Just take a few hours for yourself. Come on, get your coat. I'll let Sarah know I'll be gone for about twenty minutes."

"I can just drive myself," Bella said.

"In your condition, you might fall asleep at the wheel. This is no big deal. Grab your coat and let's go."

As if she didn't have the energy to resist, she nodded, went to the closet and pulled out her coat.

Bella opened her eyes when Hudson switched off the ignition of his truck. They were in the driveway of the ranch-style house. She must have dozed a little on the way here even though it hadn't been that long a drive. She was really that exhausted. It was the only reason she'd taken Hudson's offer seriously.

Was he really going to just drop her here and leave? That's exactly what she wanted, right?

"We're here," he said cheerily. "And a good thing,

too. I don't think that seat belt could have held you upright any longer."

"You're exaggerating."

"Not by much. Let's get you inside."

The stone-and-timber home was one story and sprawling, and it sat before her like a quiet haven. Hudson came around and opened her door. He offered his hand, and she took it to step down from the high running board. The cold air felt damp, as if snow was on its way. 'Twas the season.

As she walked beside Hudson, she felt...small. His height and broad shoulders made him tower above her. He was a substantial man, especially in his boots and suede coat with its Sherpa lining and trim. At the door, he dug into his pocket and pulled out a key. There was an overhang above the door, and as she stepped up beside Hudson, she felt as if the two of them were the only people in the world. She figured it was sleep deprivation muddling her thoughts.

He turned the key in the lock, opened another dead bolt, then pushed open the door. As soon as they stepped inside, he was pressing buttons on the security system on a panel on the wall.

The floor of the foyer was some kind of black stone. With just one look, she could tell this house was built with quality materials.

To the right, Bella caught sight of a dining room with a hand-carved oak table and chairs, and a beautiful hutch that showcased stoneware plates. Looking ahead into the center of the house, she saw an open-concept family room and kitchen.

Hudson motioned through the family room. "There are two bedrooms over that way."

Then he motioned to the left. "I've set up an office over there, and there's a master suite behind that. Where would you like to settle?"

The lone couch in the family room was upholstered in blue and rust in a chevron design and looked cushy with its back pillows for support and comfort. She didn't pay much attention to the accompanying leather recliner and wing chair with side tables and lamps. That sofa was exactly what she needed.

"That'll be fine." As soon as she reached the sofa, she took off her coat and laid it over the back. She sank down onto the couch, and it was like sitting on a cloud.

Hudson laid the key on the immense rough-hewn coffee table. "I'm going to leave you that key. I have a spare. Do you want me to set the alarm or not?"

"I don't want to set something off by mistake."

Hudson pointed to the hangings on the walls. "Clive owns some expensive art. That's why there's a security system."

"Not to mention this beautiful furniture and that huge flat-screen TV," she said, motioning to it.

Hudson chuckled. "Yeah, not to mention that." He took out a card and a pen and jotted down the alarm code. He slid it under the key ring. "I'll set the alarm. There's the code in case you need to turn it off."

"I'm not going to move," she assured him, settling back against the cushions.

A Pendleton blanket was folded over one of the side chairs. Hudson picked it up and brought it to her, spreading it out on the lower end of the couch. "Just in case you get a chill. This will warm you up."

Just looking at Hudson Jones warmed her up, but she wasn't exhausted enough to say that. She did have a few faculties about her.

"I'll come back here after the last kid's gone from the day care center and drive you back there to get your car. You have my cell number, just in case you need me for some reason."

When her gaze caught Hudson's, their kiss became a vivid memory once more. She had the feeling he was remembering it, too.

His eyes darkened. He took a step closer but then said, "The refrigerator's stocked if you get hungry. Greta takes care of that for me."

"Greta?"

"Her husband, Edmond, is the foreman on the ranch. They live in the log cabin just around the bend from the house."

After a last look at her, he turned and headed toward the door. She had the feeling if he stayed longer he could sit on that sofa beside her, and then who knew what could happen?

"See you in a few hours," he said.

She heard the beep of the alarm as he set it and the click of the door when it closed. She heard his truck revving up in the driveway and backing out. Taking one of the throw pillows from a corner of the sofa, she positioned it, curled up with her head on it and pulled up the blanket.

She saw Hudson's face in her mind's eye, right before she succumbed to her fatigue.

* * *

When Hudson returned to the Lazy B that evening, he let himself in and switched off the alarm. He'd stopped at Wings to Go, hungry himself and sure Bella was, too. Greta had left salads in the refrigerator, and they'd go great with the wings. He knew Bella would want to get home, but sleep and food and quiet had seemed to be a necessity for her today.

When he switched on the small side light in the family room, she didn't stir. He watched her from a few feet away. She was curled on her side facing the sofa, the blanket pulled up to her shoulders. He wanted nothing more than to go over to that sofa and finger her hair, touch her cheek, kiss her. Even sleeping, she awakened his appetite for more than barbecued wings.

Still, he let her sleep while he went to the kitchen and set the table for dinner. By the time he put out the salads and the wings, he heard the rustle of movement from the sofa.

"Hey, sleepyhead," he said with a smile. "Are you hungry?"

Pushing off the blanket, she sat up and tried to wipe the sleep from her eyes. "I didn't hear you come in."

"You got a good nap."

She yawned. "I did. I feel like I got more sleep than I have all week." She checked her watch. "Oh my gosh. I've got to get home. Jamie will wonder what happened to me."

"Text him. You can take another fifteen or twenty minutes to eat supper. You've got to take care of yourself, Bella. You won't be much help to him if you get run-down or sick."

She looked torn, but then she nodded. "I know you're right." She'd left her purse on the coffee table, and now she took her phone from it and quickly texted. Afterward she said, "Something smells great."

"I picked up wings. The rest of the meal was in the fridge. I'm a lucky guy."

He saw her look around as if she hadn't really done it before. He spent a lot of time in the family room. A flannel jacket lay over the top of one chair. His laptop sat on the coffee table beside an unfinished cup of coffee. Another pair of boots sat near the gas fireplace.

Standing, she started toward him. "It looks as if you've settled in."

"For now," he said, meaning it. After all, he didn't know how long his wandering spirit would keep him here. He motioned to one of the ladder-back chairs at the table. "Have a seat."

She washed up at the sink and then sat across from him, studying him rather than the food.

"What?" he asked.

"You went to an awful lot of trouble for me today. I guess I have to wonder why."

"I didn't want you dropping from exhaustion at the day care center," he said wryly, skirting the question.

Still, she kept her gaze on him. "So you'd do this for any of your employees?" She motioned to the meal and the house, and he knew what she meant.

"No, I wouldn't. You're special, Bella."

Her pretty brows arched. "Usually when a man does something like this, he wants something in return."

He put down the wing he was about to eat. "Maybe I do. That kiss just didn't happen out of the blue. There's been something simmering since we met. Don't you agree?"

She looked flustered. "I don't know what you mean. I—"

"Bella, tell me the truth. If you can honestly say you don't feel any sparks between us, I'll drop the whole thing, take you home, not approach you again with anything in my mind other than a boss-and-employee relationship."

"That's what we should have," she reminded him.

"Maybe. Are you going to answer my question?"

Stalling for time, she spooned potato salad onto her plate. Then she looked up at him with guileless brown eyes. "Yes, I feel the sparks, but I've been doing my best to ignore them."

He pushed the broccoli salad dish toward her. "That's only going to work for so long."

She sighed and took a sip of her sparkling water. Then she said, "Can we table this discussion for now?"

"Am I making you uncomfortable?"

"No. It's just I have my mind on getting home because I know Jamie's going to need my help."

"And you're afraid if we get embroiled in this type of discussion, you won't get home soon enough."

She picked up a wing. "Yes."

He nodded. "Okay, let's eat."

They were quiet as they ate but still aware of each other. Their gazes met often. Their fingers brushed when they reached for another wing at the same time. He noticed the pulse at the hollow of Bella's neck. He caught her studying the scar under his eye.

"I fell out of a tree house when I was a kid," he said, "and got scraped up pretty good."

She blushed a little. "Stitches?" she asked.

"Yep, twelve of them. How about you? Were you adventurous when you were a kid?"

She was silent for a few moments, then she said, "Not in the tree-climbing kind of way." She hesitated. "But after Jamie and I went to live with our grandparents, I was difficult—acting out, truancy, that kind of thing."

She looked as if there was a lot more to that story, but he didn't press. He just responded, "You don't look like the type. Now you seem to want to go by the book and obey every rule."

"Maybe because I stepped over the line one too many times." With that conclusion, she stood and carried her plate to the sink. Then she asked, "Can you point me to the powder room?"

He waved down the hall. "It's right across from the office."

She nodded and went that way.

He cleaned up in the kitchen, still wondering about her "acting out" escapades. When he heard her in the hall off the foyer, he met her there and pointed to the office. "Did you peek in there?"

"No."

"Not the nosy type?" he asked with a grin.

"Not usually," she answered agreeably.

"I'd like to show you the paintings in there. Come on. It will only take a minute."

He led her into the office, and when she joined him,

she gave a little gasp of pleasure. "Oh my. Are they originals?"

"They are. Clive considers Barclay the best Western painter in America."

He gave his attention to the landscape of a Montana ranch near Billings, then another near Missoula—mountains with a stream running through.

"I noticed the wall hangings in the family room right away when I walked in. They're beautiful, too. Mr. Bickler has wonderful taste and deep pockets."

"Deep pockets can't buy taste," Hudson assured her. "But, yes, Clive has both. I'm fortunate this place was available when I was looking around to find somewhere to live. I thought you might appreciate these."

"I do."

He pointed to a vase sitting on a wide windowsill. "Most of his pottery is signed, too."

She came closer to the window to examine the vase. The darkness outside and the quietness of the house wrapped them in a type of intimacy. He was very aware of the master suite right down the hall.

When Bella looked up at him, he wanted to kiss her so badly that he could remember her taste. But he didn't want to scare her away. He was afraid another kiss right now might just do that. Timing, he knew, was everything.

His voice was husky when he said, "I'll take you back to the day care center, then I'm going to follow you home to make sure you get there safely." He put his forefinger to her lips. "And don't say I don't have to do that. I know I don't. I want to."

Her lips under his finger were warm, pliable, sexy,

and he knew exactly how sweet. When he removed his finger, she was still looking at him. He suspected there was a depth to Bella that not many people probed. She kept up a wall of reserve, and that held them at bay. But he was going to break through that reserve.

One day.

A short time later, Hudson and Bella stood next to his truck at Jamie's ranch. Bella didn't know how to thank Hudson for what he'd done for her this afternoon. He confused her. She hadn't expected the kindness that seemed an innate part of his nature. She felt she had to return that kindness and maybe even take a figurative step toward him, toward admitting those sparks they both knew they felt.

"Can you come in for a few minutes?" she asked. "I'd like you to meet my brother." If Jamie saw the attraction between her and Hudson, he could help her sort it out.

There was a bright moon in the sky, and even though his face was shadowed, she caught the surprise on it. "I'd like that," he said.

And just like that, Hudson took her hand and they walked toward the door. He let go as she opened it. Inside the house, the TV was blaring. Paige Dalton Traub was on the sofa playing with Katie. Jamie was on the floor with Henry and Jared building a structure with colored blocks. He looked up when Bella came in.

"I'm glad you got some dinner," he said. "It was hit-and-miss here."

She'd texted him about the wings and eating with Hudson. She and Jamie had no secrets from each other.

Jared crawled quickly toward Bella. Bella dropped her purse, shrugged out of her coat and laid it over a chair. Then she scooped up the baby, hugging him close.

"Hi there, big boy. I hope you're not giving your dad too much trouble."

"He and Katie aren't as fussy today," Jamie said, getting to his feet and hauling Henry into his arms. "I'm hoping the teething crisis is over."

Bella introduced the two men.

They shook hands, and Bella noticed they seemed to be sizing each other up. They were about the same height and supremely fit from their outdoor work, though Hudson was a bit huskier. Then Jamie introduced Paige—Sutter Traub's wife, elementary school teacher and mom—to Hudson.

Paige said, "If you'll excuse me, I'll get this little girl started on her bath."

Jared suddenly leaned toward Hudson, holding his arms out. Not sure how Hudson would react, Bella said, "You don't have to—"

But Hudson didn't hesitate. He lifted the little boy from Bella and held him high in the air. "Hi there, big guy. I hear you've been stealing sleep from your dad and your aunt. I hope those teeth have settled down."

"Until the next one pops up," Jamie said wryly.

Hudson transferred Jared to the crook of his arm, and the little boy seemed satisfied to stay there for the moment. "I can't imagine caring for three of them," he said to Jamie with a shake of his head. "This is like having your own day care."

"I hope Bella's told you we have nothing against

Just Us Kids. But since the triplets were preemies, I don't want to take the chance of putting them in day care yet. You understand, don't you?"

"Of course I do. And they're in good hands from what I hear."

"Our helpers are the best," Jamie said. "And so is Bella," he tacked on.

It was easy to see the bond between brother and sister and the way they communicated with their eyes, with a gesture, with no words at all. Jamie deposited Henry in his play saucer and then held out his arms for Jared.

Placing him in another saucer, he said, "Come on, fella, you're going to be next for a bath."

"I'd better be going," Hudson said. "It was good to meet you."

"Likewise," Jamie agreed with a nod. And then he maneuvered the two saucers into the kitchen.

Bella walked Hudson to the door. "It's always chaos here."

"Just like the day care center," Hudson said with a smile.

They were standing very close, and neither of them seemed to want to move away. Bella wasn't sure how to say goodbye to Hudson. She wasn't sure where they were headed. They were in between a working relationship and a personal one, and she wasn't even sure she should step into the personal one. But when she looked into Hudson's eyes, she wanted to.

"Thank you for this afternoon," she said sincerely. "I needed the sleep and the quiet, and those great wings."

Hudson chuckled. "Here I thought you were going to say you needed supper with me."

"All of it was really kind of you."

Hudson reached out and touched her cheek. "It was more than kindness, Bella. Sometime we'll continue the discussion we started over dinner."

Then he was stepping away from her, opening the door and leaving. She stood in the doorway, watching him until he drove away.

She found herself disappointed he hadn't kissed her. Confusion? Thy name was Bella.

Chapter Five

On Saturday morning Hudson rose before sunrise. After downing a protein shake along with one of Greta's cinnamon rolls, he went for a ride on Breeze, contemplating his day. He considered what Bella had said about purpose and realized except for handling the day care's PR problems, he didn't have one. He thought about last evening, meeting Jamie and watching him handle the triplets, as well as his ranch. The guy needed more than a baby chain. Since he'd noticed fencing on Jamie's ranch that needed to be repaired, Hudson decided what he was going to do with his day before bad weather moved in. Throughout his adult life, he'd never had to consult anyone when he wanted to go somewhere or do something. So he didn't now.

He drove his truck to the lumberyard, bought the supplies he needed and headed out to the Stockton ranch, down a rutted road on the side field. The ground was frozen, so he couldn't repost fence. But he could replace slats and make repairs that would keep cattle in and horses safe.

Before 9 a.m. he was working on the fence line, the

physical labor feeling good. He'd missed it. After an hour, he sat inside his truck, warmed up with another cinnamon roll, then went back at it. It was noon when he spotted Jamie rushing out the back of the house and across the field. Hudson didn't at all expect the reaction he got when Jamie was within earshot of him.

The rancher asked, "What are you doing out here?"

"I thought you needed help with the fence line. You don't want your cattle or horses getting out, do you?"

Hudson could see the angry expression on Jamie Stockton's face now that he was closer. "Of course I don't want them getting out. But I don't want *you* doing my work."

"I was trying to help out, just like the baby chain helps you with the triplets."

Jamie's words puffed white in the almost frigid air. "That's different. I have to accept help so Katie, Henry and Jared stay healthy and happy and content. But as far as the ranch goes, I can handle it on my own. Did Bella tell you I needed help out here?"

"No," Hudson said honestly and quickly. "I saw it when we drove by. Your fence slats are falling off. Your posts are leaning. I would have helped with those, but I can't with the ground frozen. If the snow rots them and takes them down, you might have to put up something temporary."

"That's *my* worry, not yours."

To top things off, Hudson caught sight of Bella running toward them. He could see she hadn't even taken time to zip her parka. She jogged toward them and came to an abrupt stop. When she did, he saw how troubled she looked. He hadn't meant to make things harder for her or for her brother.

He addressed Jamie again. "I understand if you want me to stop. But I already bought the supplies. What if I unload them in your barn?"

"I don't need charity," Jamie insisted stubbornly. "You can take your planks and nails and leave."

Bella went to her brother and put her hand on his arm. "Jamie."

"I mean it, Jones," Jamie said tersely. "You took over the day care center under Bella's nose when she'd done nothing wrong. Maybe you had to because you were invested in it. But you have no investment here. Just let me and mine take care of ourselves."

Hudson knew about pride. Walker had been the big brother who bailed Hudson out of scrapes and then tried to tell him what to do. Hudson had always balked and his pride got in the way of a good relationship with Walker.

Jamie had lost his wife. He had to juggle more than a man should have to. At the end of the day, his pride was a valuable asset.

So Hudson didn't argue with him. He just tipped his Stetson to Bella, nodded to Jamie and said, "I understand. I'm out of here."

He gathered up the few supplies he had lying about and stowed them in the back of the truck. When he stole a glance at Bella, he saw she was caught in the middle. He wouldn't want to be in her position. She had to support her brother, and if that meant watching him turn down help, then that's what she had to do.

Hudson climbed in his truck, and as he drove away,

he peered into the rearview mirror. Bella looked appalled that he was leaving like this. But he'd had no choice. He'd miscalculated badly. What was that old saying? *No good deed goes unpunished.*

He'd found that out today. Wandering, rambling, not being connected to anyone seemed to be the easier road to take. Yet he realized now it might be a road that no longer satisfied him, a road that had kept him from forming real connections and friendships.

The Monday morning influx of babies and children under the age of five was the ultimate mayhem. But somehow Bella managed it and kept everybody, from parents to kids to teachers, smiling when she did it.

Hudson hadn't had a chance to talk to her, and he wasn't sure she'd want to talk to him. Now when he looked back on what he'd done, he saw how it could be misconstrued. His actions could be considered high-handed, arrogant, maybe even condescending. She might want to stay far away from him. So he was surprised when, after the last child was logged in for the morning, Bella came to his office and rapped on the open door.

He stood and came around his desk, not wanting a barrier between them. It seemed as if they had enough of those, though he wasn't even sure what some of them were.

"I wanted to talk to you," she said, looking as if she had something serious on her mind.

"I wanted to talk to *you*," he returned.

They were about two feet apart, and Bella looked lovely today in a pale blue sweater and navy slacks.

She'd worn boots, too, no doubt in anticipation of the snow that was predicted for later. It seemed Bella was the type who liked to be prepared.

They both said "I'm sorry" at the same time. He stopped and waved at her to go first. "Go ahead," he said. "But you have nothing to be sorry for."

"I'm sorry for Jamie's behavior," she apologized.

"His behavior was my fault," Hudson assured her.

Shaking her head vigorously, she responded, "No, it wasn't. One thing I've learned is that we have to own our actions. Jamie simply overreacted. It was a wonderful thing you tried to do."

Hudson stuffed his hands in his pockets so he didn't think as much about reaching out and touching her. "*Wonderful* didn't turn out so well."

"It's nothing against you, Hudson. Jamie's already accepting so much help with the triplets, he's touchy about it. He feels as if his life is running him instead of him running his life. Do you know what I mean?"

Thinking about what she'd said, he nodded. "Yes, I do. I can see the responsibilities he has sitting on his shoulders. They're wearing him down. I think they're wearing you down a bit, too."

"I'm fine," she assured him. "But I am worried about Jamie. I had a break on Friday, thanks to you. I really needed that afternoon nap. *And* that dinner. But Jamie won't take a break."

"Maybe he feels if he does, everything will fall apart. I should have discussed fixing that fence with him before I did it. I never meant to cause such a ruckus."

"You did fix the worst part, and whether he realizes it or not, he's going to be grateful when he thinks about it." She took a step closer to Hudson, and he felt his heart beating faster.

Before he realized what she was going to do, she stood on tiptoe and kissed him on the cheek. That kiss was as light as the touch of a butterfly's wings, but he felt it in every fiber of his being.

When she stepped away, she said simply, "Thank you," and then she was gone from his office.

Hudson brushed his fingers over the place on his cheek where her lips had touched his skin.

He did that often over the next hour, aware that he'd been touched by that gesture as he hadn't by anything in a long time.

Throughout the morning, he found himself staring out the window more than at his computer. Around noon he watched the first snowflakes begin to fall. They didn't start lightly but multiplied quickly, coating the grass and the pavement in no time.

The phone began ringing, and he knew why. Parents would want to pick up their kids early. To his surprise, every single one of them did. Usually there were stragglers but not today. And that gave Hudson an idea.

After the teachers had left, Bella was reaching for her parka in the break room when he found her there and asked, "How would you like to go riding in the snow?"

She zipped up her parka. "Are you serious?"

"I am. If you're game, I'll follow you to your brother's, where I can apologize to him for my high-handedness, then we can go for a short ride and chase the snowflakes. What do you think?"

"At your place?"

"Yeah, at my place. There's a horse who will be perfect for you, a little chestnut named Boots. She's got four white ones."

Bella laughed. "Okay, I'm game. Let's go."

A short time later, they pulled up at Jamie's ranch. He parked behind Bella and walked up to the door with her. She opened it, went inside and called "Jamie? Somebody's with me who'd like to talk to you."

Jamie came from the kitchen, his finger over his lips. "Not too loud. All three of them are napping. I think it's a first. Country Kids let out early, and Fallon's upstairs sorting the triplets' clothes. Some of them are already too small."

As Jamie spotted Hudson, he went silent. But Hudson didn't hesitate to walk right up to the man.

"I'm sorry," he said. "I never meant to overstep. You want to run your ranch and your life your way. I get that. I should have talked to you before I brought in supplies and did anything."

Jamie was silent as he studied Hudson, maybe trying to figure out if he was being sincere. Then he extended his hand. "No hard feelings. You did a good job and saved me a lot of work. But I want the bill for those supplies and the time you put in."

"How about if we split it down the middle? I'll give you the bill for the supplies, but my time was free."

Bella's brother considered Hudson's words, then he nodded. "All right. But I owe you one. If you need a favor for something, you come to me."

"Deal," Hudson said with a grin. "For right now,

though, I'd like to take your sister riding in the snow at my place. Is that all right with you?"

Cocking his head, Jamie seemed to weigh what Bella might want.

She said, "I'd like to go if you don't need me. Is Fallon going to stick around?"

"She is. She said she can stay the night if need be."

"I'm just going to change into warmer clothes. I'll be quick—five minutes."

As Bella hurried up the steps, Jamie murmured, "Riding in the snow. We did that when we were kids."

"Before your grandparents took you in?" Hudson asked, still curious about Bella's upbringing.

"Oh, yeah, before they took us in. After that, we didn't have a whole lot of fun."

"Bella told me they didn't want you. I can't believe that."

"Oh, believe it, because it was true. I'm surprised she talked to you about it. She never talks about our childhood. Did she tell you anything else?"

"Just that she believed her grandfather blamed the two of you for your grandmother's death."

"True, too, and he might have been right."

The way Jamie was looking at him, Hudson wondered if he expected him to go on, to say more that Bella might have told him. But there wasn't anything else. Now Hudson was even more curious.

He forgot about Bella's past, though, when she came rushing down the stairs in jeans, riding boots and a pretty pink-and-white turtleneck sweater. He had a sudden urge to cuddle her in his arms. To be honest, he actually wanted to do more than that. But the cuddling sure would be nice, too.

She grabbed her parka and made sure she had her gloves and hat.

"Let's go," he said. "I'll call Edmond on the way, and he can get the horses saddled up."

As Bella rode beside Hudson in his truck, she wasn't sure what had made her agree to this crazy proposal. Maybe it was Hudson's enjoyment of the idea. Maybe it was his enthusiasm. Maybe she just needed a little fun in her life.

Hudson didn't pull into the driveway at the house but rather drove farther down the lane and pulled over at a big red barn. She spotted a log cabin not far away.

"Is that where the foreman lives?"

"Yes. It's a homey place. Greta's into crafts as well as cooking. I think you'd like it. Maybe we can stop there afterward."

At the door to the barn, snowflakes swirled lazily around them as Bella said, "I feel guilty for leaving Jamie back there with the triplets."

"They're his kids, Bella, not yours."

For a moment, she was almost angry at the remark, and Hudson must have seen that. "I'm sorry. I shouldn't have been so blunt. But it's true. At some point he's going to have to be able to handle his own life. He said Fallon was there, so you don't have to worry about him, at least not for the next few hours."

"You can look at the situation pragmatically. I can't."

He took a step closer to her and held her by the

shoulders. "Someone has to. Maybe I can help you find a balance."

"And what can I do for you?"

The way Hudson was looking at her, she knew exactly what she could do for him, and it involved a kiss. She kept perfectly still, but he didn't bend his head. He didn't squeeze her tighter.

Rather he said, "Not everything's a negotiation, Bella. I meant it with Jamie when I said I don't want anything in return, and I mean it with you, too. I just enjoy being with you. Maybe that will work to both our advantages."

"How's that?"

"You think I need purpose in my life. Maybe I'll get a better sense of that by being around you."

"Sometimes, Hudson, I can't tell if you're making fun of me or if you're serious."

"I will never make fun of you, Bella. You're a beautiful, intelligent woman who deserves to be listened to. Why would I want to make fun of that?"

A snowflake landed on her nose, but she didn't care, didn't move. Suddenly it had become more important that Hudson understand her and where she'd been, at least part of it. So she explained.

"My parents were great, at least what I can remember. I have some pictures of them in an album. Thank goodness, our grandparents let us keep those. In those photos, Mom and Dad were laughing and playing ball with us, and even jumping under the hose on a hot summer day. We felt listened to…important…loved. But after my parents were gone, my grandparents talked only to each other. They made decisions with each other. They never consulted us. They sent—"

She stopped. She wasn't going to tell him about the brothers and sisters they never saw. She didn't want him to feel sorry for her. She just wanted him to know the way it had been and why she reacted sometimes now the way she did. "My grandparents just didn't listen, and after Grandma died, my grandfather shut off. It was as if he wasn't even there. He put food on the table. He barked orders at us. But he was never kind the way a parent should be kind. He was never there to listen to what happened at school or after school. He was cold and hard, and I couldn't wait to leave."

Now Hudson did put his arms around her. The brim of his Stetson kept snow from falling on her face. He admitted, "I know about cold parents. My mother's that way. But she calls it reserved. It comes down to the same thing."

"I think Gramps was born that way. Then when he was in a situation he didn't want to be in, burdened with us, he withdrew more into himself. Why do you think your mom was cold?"

"I'm not sure. My guess is she wasn't happy in the marriage. When you're not happy, when the other person doesn't try to make you happy, what's left but resentment and maybe even contempt? That's always what I felt vibrating between them."

"But you had your brothers."

"Yes, I did. We established our own rules, kept each other safe, fought, yelled, but told each other our secrets."

"Like brothers should. Is that why you helped Walker when he needed you?"

"That's one of the reasons."

He brushed snowflakes from her hair, and the stroke of his hands almost made her purr. "Let's get you inside before you become a snow woman."

She laughed, and he opened the barn door for her.

"Edmond, how goes it?" Hudson called when he saw his foreman in one of the stalls.

"Just getting Boots ready. Your Breeze is champing at the bit. She can't wait to get out there."

"They might not be so happy once that snow's falling all around them. But we won't keep them out long."

"Greta wants to know if you'd like to come to supper when you get back. She has a huge pot of chili on the stove, and she says it's just what you'll need after a ride in the snow."

Hudson looked at Bella. "Do you think Jamie can do without you?"

She considered everything Hudson had said about having her own life, about Jamie needing a life of his own, too. Yet she knew right now their lives had converged. Still, Fallon was helping him, and she said she'd even stay the night. Bella had the feeling that Fallon wanted to spend as much time as she could with Jamie. Maybe it was a good thing if she stayed away for a little while.

"Let me give him a call and make sure before we saddle up."

The call took only a few minutes, and she was ready to mount Boots. Hudson stood next to the pretty horse holding its reins. "What did he say?"

"He said I should have supper here with you. Everything is under control back there."

"Good. I lowered the stirrup a bit so you could mount easier. Once you're up, I'll fix it for you."

He could have just given her a leg up, but she was glad he'd done it this way instead. Hudson's touch made her skittish, and maybe he knew that. What she'd heard about Hudson, about him being a love-'em-and-leave-'em cowboy, just didn't mesh with who he really was. She'd found him to be a gentleman, and she liked that. She liked it a lot.

She'd been right about the way Hudson sat on a horse. His back was straight and his shoulders square. Yet his body had enough flexibility that he seemed one with the horse. He looked as if he'd been made for riding. And he looked incredibly handsome, especially against the snow that frosted the landscape.

She followed Hudson since he knew the terrain better than she did. Besides that, she trusted him to lead. Odd that she thought of that now. She hadn't trusted him when he'd first come to Just Us Kids, but she'd learned better. Her experience with men—other than her brother—had been anything but positive. Trusting seemed as far away as dreaming or loving someone who would love you back forever.

The atmosphere out here was positively church-like. The tall pines, the hushed silence, the pure whiteness of fresh snow. Bella felt herself relaxing into the moment, simply enjoying being alive.

Hudson suddenly changed direction and gestured for her to follow him due south. They rode along a copse of pine and aspen and rounded a corner. She felt a gasp come from her soul when she saw a pond before her with white softness edging its borders. The water reflected the gray sky, but there were places where it picked up sparkle from somewhere.

Hudson waited for her to ride up beside him, then he asked, "Are you game to dismount for a while? Those trees will protect us from the snow." He motioned to a canopy that looked like a little haven.

"Sure," she said, giving him a smile. "It's beautiful out here."

He gave a nod and then dismounted first so he could give her a hand. She would have just jumped off her horse, but Hudson was right there, his hands on her waist, helping her to the ground. He lifted her down, and she felt like air in his arms. There was strength there and a sure grip that assured her she wouldn't fall.

He took hold of their horse's leads. They walked about twenty feet into the copse of trees, and she saw immediately why he'd wanted to bring her here. It was a more in-depth view of the lake, the snow on the reeds, the white birch on the far shore, the pine canopy that kept snow from falling on them.

"Sometimes we don't realize how much noise surrounds us all day until we're in a quiet place like this."

"Do you come here often?" she asked, almost in a whisper because that seemed fitting here.

"I do. I have that luxury because I don't have to take care of triplets when I go home."

Facing him, she asked, "Are you trying to make a point?"

He gazed down at her with sincerity in his eyes.

"Nope. Just attempting to show you the other side of having a purpose."

She felt mesmerized by him...so drawn to him. "I think you have a purpose when you come out here."

"What would that be?"

"To connect with something outside yourself, something bigger than yourself. My guess is you find here what many people find in meditation or in church."

"Wide-open space has always meant freedom to me. I don't like fences or boundaries that predict where I have to stay."

That statement prompted her to probe deeper. "Do you think you were *born* to be a risk taker or an adventurer? Or did you learn it?"

"I only take calculated risks. And as far as being born an adventurer, I'd say I learned it, in order to escape my siblings and my parents."

"I wish I had gone that route," she admitted with a sigh, and then was appalled she'd said it. What she didn't want to do was get into her background. What she didn't want to do was explain what had happened when she was a teenager rebelling against her grandparents who didn't love her, against fate that had taken her parents from her, along with her other siblings, too.

Apparently Hudson's thoughts ran in another direction from her teenage years because he turned to face her, adjusted the chin strap on her hat and said, "You can still be an adventurer. It's never too late to start."

The darkening of his eyes, the heat she suddenly felt between them, the vibrations that were all about male and female awareness made her ask jokingly, "You mean I should catch a plane to Paris?"

"No," he said honestly. "I was thinking that you should kiss me again."

When Hudson wrapped his arms around her, she didn't hesitate to let him pull her close. He dragged his thumb down her cheek and kissed the trail his finger had taken. His sensual touch sent tremors through her, and in spite of herself, she envisioned them naked in his bed. She should have stopped the thought right there. If she had, when his lips sealed to hers, maybe then she wouldn't have felt like melting into his body. The cold seemed to swell around them, but they were warm, getting hot, even hotter. His lips seemed to burn hers, and when his tongue breached her lips, forged into her mouth, took the kiss deeper and wetter, she wrapped her arms around his neck and held on for dear life.

Hudson stopped the kiss suddenly...didn't end it... just stopped it.

She knew he wanted another one because he kissed along her lower lip, then the corner of her mouth. After a deep breath, he said, "You make me feel too much."

"You make me shake," she admitted.

His soft chuckle said he liked that idea, and he came back for another kiss, and then another until time didn't matter. The swish of pine boughs didn't matter. Snow mounting around their boots didn't matter. Only Hudson's desire, his hands at the nape of her neck and his body heat mattered.

He broke away again, then he looked down at her, breathing hard. He assured her, "If we were someplace else, someplace warmer and more comfortable, we'd be doing more than kissing."

But we shouldn't be, a voice inside her yelled. *Why not?* echoed back. She ignored both and said to Hudson, "I'm not sure we *know* what we're doing."

"That's the fun of it—the adventure of it," he reminded her. "Let's just see where this goes, Bella." Just in case her response wasn't what he wanted to hear, he brushed her lips with his again and wrapped his arm around her. "I think that chili at Greta and Edmond's is good and done. Let's go get a bowl and warm up."

She didn't need chili to warm up. She'd been plenty warm when Hudson had been kissing her. She had a feeling she'd be plenty warm every time she thought about it, too. Could she be an adventurer and take it further?

Thank goodness, she didn't have to answer that question now.

Chapter Six

As soon as Bella walked into Greta and Edmond's house, she felt as if she were surrounded by warmth, and not just warmth coming from the woodstove. Whereas Clive Bickler's house was decorated with expensive paintings, fine-quality wall hangings and artist-signed pottery, Greta and Edmond's little house was simple and cozy. It was a log home, and Greta had kept the country look about it.

Everything was spick-and-span, shiny and authentic. The wide-plank flooring was worn. The living room's magnificently colored, large Southwestern rug needed repair in one corner and wore a straggling fringe in the other. The appliances weren't state-of-the-art, but Bella could tell they were used and used well. The colors migrating through the cabin—whether the fabric was striped, flowered or solid—were burgundy, green and yellow.

"I love your house," Bella told Greta. "It's charming."

Greta motioned to the curtains and the valances. "I made those myself. I still have an old treadle machine that works just fine. We managed to save it from the flood."

Edmond motioned to the table where a crock full of chili sat in the center. "Take a seat and we can talk while we eat."

"Our ranch was almost wiped out," Greta told Bella. "We saved what livestock we could first, then a few other things like my sewing machine, photo albums, framed pictures, a set of dishes my grandma handed down. But that was it. Everything else was wiped out when the house filled with water up to the second floor."

Edmond sat next to his wife and covered her hand with his. It was obvious that thinking about the flood was still an emotional experience for the couple.

Bella stole a glance at Hudson. He was watching Greta and Edmond, obviously trying to understand.

Greta's husband went on to explain, "We were living in the boardinghouse, not knowing what we were going to do next. No job, not much in the way of possessions. We basically had each other. We could have gone to live with our kids, but we didn't want to do that. They have their own lives. I was using my phone every day to search for jobs and not coming up with anything because lots of folks in town were in the same boat."

"But then fate stepped in, I guess," Greta said. "The owner of the Lazy B wanted to leave Rust Creek Falls, didn't think it would ever come to life again, and Clive Bickler saw the good deal that it was. Edmond and I had helped organize one of the old barns that wasn't underwater where we could give out supplies to people who needed it—bottled water, blankets, some clothes.

Clive heard about that somehow, and the fact that Edmond knew horses and cows. So he asked us if we'd manage his place, room and board free. It was a deal we couldn't refuse. We just hope he never sells the place."

During the next hour, Greta and Edmond were full of lively stories about times on their own ranch when they'd had it, as well as this one. Eventually, Edmond and Hudson got to talking about horses while Bella and Greta spoke of good meals to make on the go. Bella was thoroughly enjoying herself and could see why Hudson liked spending time with these people. As a couple they were cute together, bumping each other's shoulders, touching each other often, and Bella could tell from the sparkle in their eyes that they were still deeply in love.

They were eating dessert, a delicious gingerbread with whipped cream, when Greta and Edmond exchanged a look. Edmond nodded, and Greta addressed Hudson.

"We have some really great news."

Hudson gave a chuckle. "What would that be? You can't make me any more food than you already do. It won't fit in the refrigerator or on the counter."

Greta waved his comment away. "This has to do with our children."

Edmond added, "One specifically. Our daughter Gracie is pregnant. She and Cole are overjoyed, and so are we."

Greta cut in, "Edmond can't wait to teach a little one how to ride a horse."

Hudson said to Bella, "Their daughter lives in Kalispell, so they'll be able to see their grandchild often."

"A little girl," Greta said with glee. "Can you imagine? Bows and pigtails and shiny shoes."

Edmond shook his head. "Not if she's a tomboy like Gracie was."

Bella saw Greta's and Edmond's radiant faces, and Hudson's happiness for them. She felt happy for them, too. "A baby is something glorious to look forward to," she said, and she meant it.

But inside she felt as if the evening had suddenly wilted because reality had struck again. These good people had reminded her what family was all about—meeting someone you loved, getting married, having kids. A sudden sadness washed over her, especially when she thought about her kiss with Hudson and what it could mean...what it *did* mean. They were so attracted to each other, and if she let that kiss go further, the next time—

There shouldn't be a next time. If they started a relationship, it couldn't go anywhere. No man wanted her because she couldn't have kids. She could not carry a baby to term. When would she finally let that reality take hold?

Maybe she could find love later in life, she told herself. When she was fifty? When having kids didn't matter to a man? Was that ever the case? She knew what Hudson was like with kids. She'd seen it over and over again. He enjoyed them. He could get down on their level. He could even *be* one at times. He would want children.

Somehow she managed to be part of Edmond and Greta's conversation, talking about kids, toys and even the day care center. She managed to smile and share in their excitement. But deep down, she hurt. That hurt would never go away.

Hudson was confused as he drove Bella home. They'd had a marvelous afternoon. Their ride had been romantic and fun—the snow falling around them, riding together, the grove in the trees that had sheltered them while they'd kissed. He knew he hadn't been mistaken about Bella being as involved in it as he was.

Dinner with Edmond and Greta had seemed to be enjoyable, too. But then suddenly, he could tell there'd been a change in Bella. She'd grown quieter, though not a lot quieter. He'd only noticed her gaze hadn't met his as often. There had been a tension there when he'd spoken to her, even about something as mundane as a child's toy. And he wanted to get to the bottom of it.

He felt as if he'd done something terribly wrong. Maybe once that wouldn't have bothered him so much, but this was Bella, and it did bother him.

When he arrived at the Stockton ranch and parked in the drive, he hadn't even turned off the ignition when Bella said, "You don't have to walk me to the door. I'll be fine."

That almost made him angry. He switched off the motor and said, "That sidewalk looks slippery. I'll walk you to the door." He knew his firmness brooked no argument.

Bella seemed to accept his decision, but she didn't

look happy about it. She didn't wait for him to come around to her door. She opened it herself and hopped down.

When he rounded the truck, she was already on her way to the door. His legs were a lot longer than hers, and he caught up easily. He clasped her elbow and made sure she wasn't going to slip on the walk. At the porch she turned to him, and it seemed that she steeled herself to meet his gaze.

She smiled and said, "Thank you for today. I had a lovely time."

She'd said the words, but there was some kind of underlying message in them that he didn't like and he didn't accept. It was as if this was the last time they were going to have a lovely time.

"Bella, what's wrong?"

"Nothing's wrong," she said with a little too much vehemence.

"I don't believe that. Everything was fine, and then suddenly it wasn't. I want to know what's going on in that head of yours."

She gave him an almost defiant look that said maybe he didn't have the right to know what was going on in her head. She was correct about that, so he tried a different tack.

"If I did something wrong, I'd like to know what it was."

Now the defiance was gone, and she looked genuinely concerned. "Hudson, you didn't do anything wrong. I enjoyed the ride, I really did. And Greta and Edmond are a wonderful couple. I can see why you like spending time with them."

"But?" he prompted.

She shook her head. "No *buts*. It's just that our situation hasn't changed. You're my boss. I think we should keep our relationship colleague to colleague."

Settling his thumb under her chin, he tipped her face up and studied her. That might have been one of her concerns, but it wasn't the only one. Still he couldn't force her to confide in him. All he could do was try to gently persuade her with actions rather than words.

"We're more than colleagues, Bella. Deep down you know that."

Reluctantly he took his thumb away from her soft skin. Reluctantly he took a step back. "But I respect what you're saying. I respect you."

He turned to go. "I'll see you at Just Us Kids." Then suddenly he stopped and looked over his shoulder at her. "If you ever want to change our colleague status, just say so. I'm flexible." He left her standing on the porch contemplating his words.

As he climbed into his truck, he saw her step inside. He just hoped that someday soon she would confide in him what was bothering her.

Because if she didn't, they would just remain colleagues…until he left Rust Creek Falls.

On Tuesday afternoon, Bella stopped in Hudson's office. They hadn't had contact all day, and he was glad to see her now. She motioned to the classrooms.

"All the children are gone early for a change. We had a light day with the snow keeping some of the kids home. So I'm going to scoot. I called Jazzy, and I'm going out to the ranch to shoot photos. I have about an hour and half of daylight. With the snow and the sun on the horizon, I should be able to get some good shots."

"After I close up, do you want company?" he asked.

"I might be finished by the time you get there," she said. Then she paused and gave him a small smile. "You can help convince Jazzy that if she doesn't like the photos, she doesn't have to take any. So sure, come on out."

Because of Bella's attitude toward a relationship, he didn't want to push. But he wasn't beyond coaxing a little. Just being around her would help convince them both exactly what they should or shouldn't do. Besides, he still wanted to find out what had happened at dinner last night, and why she'd turned suddenly...*sad.* That was the only word he could find to describe her mood.

After Bella left, he finished up some work, chatted with the teachers, then when they left, he made sure the facility was locked up tight. As he drove to Brooks and Jazzy's ranch, he felt energized at the idea of seeing Bella again. Had other women ever done that to him? Sure, he'd looked forward to dates, to finding satisfaction in the most physical way. But the idea of seeing Bella again just...lightened him. That was the only way he could put it, and he felt almost happy.

He didn't think about happiness often. He just lived his life. It was one of those things that if you searched for it you couldn't find it. But he'd figured out happiness had nothing to do with what he owned. It had something to do with where he went. Maybe that's why he traveled. This lightness he felt around Bella, however, was something different altogether.

At the ranch he parked beside Bella's car. Climbing

out, he adjusted his Stetson and headed for a purple-coated figure standing at the corral fence.

Jazzy was staring into the pasture where Bella was shuffling through the snow, crouching down to get a shot, then standing to take a long view of another horse. He and Jazzy watched her as their breaths puffed white every time they breathed out. Bella wouldn't want to be out here too long in this cold, but she was dressed for it with practical boots and a parka, a scarf and knit cap. He couldn't see her expression from this distance, but her stance said she was intent on what she was doing.

"She's good with the horses," Jazzy said.

As he watched her approach one of the animals and hold out her hand, maybe with a treat, the horse nuzzled her palm. She stroked his neck and put her face close to his.

"As good as she is with kids," Hudson noted. He could feel Jazzy's gaze on him as he watched Bella.

"You like her," Jazzy said, as if it were a foregone conclusion.

"You mean it shows?"

"If someone's looking," Jazzy answered. "It's in the way you look at her. The thing is, I've heard rumors that you don't stick around very long. Are you planning to settle in Rust Creek Falls?"

"No." The word popped out of his mouth before he thought better of it. "I'm going to be moving on soon. Walker can easily find someone else to oversee the day care center."

"That might not be as easy as you think. Rust Creek Falls isn't teeming with cowboys like you with managerial experience. I hear you've done a magnificent job of getting the business back on track since the lawsuit."

"I hope that's the case. It's hard to wipe out the impression of something gone wrong. But we're steadily signing up new clients, and the old ones are staying. That's what's important."

"Do you find what you're doing fulfilling?"

He thought about it. Then he said with a shrug, "Kids or horses. That's a tough decision to make. I sure do miss being outdoors, though, working with horses most of the day."

"So you like Clive's ranch?"

"Oh, I do."

"Do you really want to move on?"

"It's my nature," he said quickly, as if he had to convince himself of that, too.

Instead of focusing on Bella, Jazzy turned to him and looked him deep in the eye. "Maybe it's only your nature until something or someone convinces you to stay."

Jazzy's words were still echoing in his mind a half hour later as Bella waved to them that she was finished and came over to the fence, her camera swinging around her neck on its strap. She climbed the crossbars and swung her leg over the top.

Jazzy said, "I'll start inside and make us hot chocolate. Maybe we can thaw out our fingers and toes."

Hudson held out his hands to Bella. She hesitated only a moment, and then she took them and let him help her down. They glanced at each other now and then on the walk to the house but didn't speak. Hudson wanted to ask her how she thought the shoot went, but he knew she wouldn't answer, not until she got a look at those photos on more than her camera screen. And he had an idea.

"Did you bring along the cord to hook your camera up to the TV?"

"Brooks and Jazzy have a smart TV?"

"Oh, I'm sure they do. We'll check when we get inside. That way you can see what the pictures look like."

"I brought my laptop," Bella said.

"Wouldn't you rather see them spread across fifty-two inches?"

She laughed. "It's a guy thing, isn't it? Having a huge TV."

Hudson stopped and studied her. "Is that a sexist remark?"

"No, it's the truth," she said.

"You don't want to watch a chick flick on fifty-two inches?"

"When I watch a chick flick, it's for the content. I don't care how big the screen is."

He just shook his head. "Venus and Mars."

"You think men and women are from two different planets?"

"I think they have two entirely different perspectives on the world."

"You might be right."

They were no sooner inside than Jazzy brought hot chocolate and sandwiches into the living room and set the tray on the coffee table.

Brooks grinned. "Perfect."

He wasn't looking at the food, though. He was staring at his wife. Her cheeks were rosy, her hair mussed. She was wearing slim jeans, boots and a heavy sweater.

"You were out there a long while," he said. "I'll switch on the gas fireplace. Extra heat won't hurt."

After Hudson and Bella had taken off their coats, scarves and hats, they came to sit down, too. Bella rubbed her hands in front of the fire. "That feels nice. I like the idea of not having to carry in the wood."

"It has an automatic pilot, too," Jazzy said, "so if the electricity goes out, we still have its heat. I imagine Clive has something like this," she said to Hudson.

"Yes, he does. It's come in handy the past few nights. No reason to put the heat up in the whole house when I'm just in one room."

Bella gave him a glance that said she was surprised he was economical about it. He had the feeling she underestimated him on a lot of things—his reputation, maybe his brother's sentiments about him, that he was a drifter and didn't settle down long in one place. Yet Walker was probably right.

Not wanting to think about that, he asked Brooks, "Can we hook Bella's camera up to your TV? Then we can all view the pictures on there."

"Without me previewing them first?" Bella asked, sounding nervous about it.

"Up to you," he said.

She chewed on her lower lip for a minute and then said, "I think I got a couple of pretty good shots. Let's do it."

After Brooks and Hudson accomplished the hookup, they all viewed the photos, one by one.

Hudson heard Jazzy's intake of breath at a photo of

a light-colored bay against the sun setting on the horizon and glinting off the snow. He hoped that meant she liked it. There were so many others to like, too. Jazzy took a few steps back so she could get a better perspective and silently watched as one photo after another appeared on the big screen. She oohed over the one of the chestnut near the pine grove when the light was still full. She aahed over a blue sky as a backdrop against pristine snow and a gray equine beauty. Bella hadn't captured only the horses, but the ranch, too. He'd seen her run from one end of the corral to the other, snapping an action shot of three horses together, but then also taking her time, sitting on a fence, snapping barns and trees and Montana's big sky.

After they viewed the photos twice, Brooks said, "Bella, these are fabulous, absolutely fabulous. I don't know how we're going to decide which ones to use."

"You don't have to decide now. I'd like to edit them a bit and do some cropping. I can send you the files."

"I have a photo printer at Clive's place," Hudson said. "Why don't we go back there and print them out. Then you can look at the printed photo as well as the digital file and decide which ones you want on the pamphlet. That might give you a better idea."

Brooks and Jazzy exchanged a look. "That sounds good to us," he said. "Now, let's have another round of hot chocolate."

Bella called Jamie to make sure everything was all right there. He said he had it under control and Fallon was keeping him company. Bella told him about the photo shoot and how Jazzy and Brooks seemed to like her photos. He was excited for her, and she saw that both of them needed something in their lives other than babies and diapers and laundry. She was glad Fallon was there with him.

An hour later they finally left for the Lazy B.

As they stepped inside, she asked, "Why do you have a photo printer?"

"I like gizmos and tech stuff, not just saddles and boots," he told her. "And I've been here long enough to have a collection. I have a camera, too. I sightsee now and then. I've gone out to the falls near Falls Mountain and taken a few shots, but mostly I use it for the day care center. My phone camera is fine, but I get better light with a point-and-shoot. If I see something that can be improved on at Just Us Kids, I take a picture so that I have a reminder of it. It's my way of working."

She followed him into the great room and took off her parka. "I'll pay you for the cost of printing the photos."

"Nonsense. I got you this commission, so to speak. It's my contribution."

As she walked with him to the study, she said, "You're a generous man, Hudson. Have you found people take advantage of that?"

"The ones who need the generosity don't. If somebody does, I chalk it up to experience learned. Giving usually isn't wasted. You give, too. You're generous with your time and your spirit, Bella. I'm sure your brother would attest to that."

When Hudson gave her compliments, Bella wasn't sure what to say. So she said nothing. As they sat next to each other at the desktop computer, their arms brushed. She didn't pull away. Being with Hudson was both unsettling and exciting. The exciting part coaxed her to let it continue. She knew she was headed for deep water and it was quite possible that she'd drown. But the attraction to Hudson was heady, like nothing she'd ever felt before. And she liked dwelling in it for just a little while.

The computer monitor was large enough to do the photos justice. When Hudson downloaded them, all the recent photos on the camera went into the program. He took a long time studying several of them that were taken at area barns and ranches.

"You're really good, Bella, even better than you know. I can frame any one of these for a wall grouping and it would stand out as artistic and meaningful."

"You're too kind," she said.

He turned toward her and pushed a strand of her hair behind her ear. "No, I'm not kind, not about this, not about you. I don't have kindness on my mind when I look at you."

"Hudson," she said on a slightly warning note.

He dropped his hand from her hair, leaned back and sighed. "You don't have to say anything else. I know how you feel about…everything. I can't say you're wrong…unless you want to enjoy the moment. Unless living for today means as much as living for tomorrow."

"Have you used that line before?" she asked, staring directly into his eyes. She knew Hudson was experienced. She knew he'd been around the block, so to speak. She knew he knew what he was doing.

For a moment she thought he was going to get angry, but then he rolled his chair away from hers. "It's not a line. It's just the way I think. It's the way I live. I'm not sure what you think my history is with women, Bella, but I don't need lines."

"No ego there," she murmured.

His serious face turned light, and he chuckled. "I never said I was a humble man. Come on, let's get these printed out. Then I'm going to follow you home to make sure you get there safely."

"No, Hudson. There's no need for that. I don't need a protector."

There must have been something in her voice that convinced him of that, but he was still a negotiator.

"All right. I won't follow you home if you promise to call me when you get there."

"I'll text you," she bargained.

He rolled his eyes but responded, "Deal."

Yet somehow, even though Bella had felt like she'd gotten her way, she knew that Hudson Jones would have the last word.

Chapter Seven

Bella found herself humming a Christmas carol the following morning as she sat at her computer at the day care center. The holiday was still weeks away, but timing didn't dampen her mood. Nor did the statistics she was examining and organizing for a year-end report.

The photo shoot yesterday had gone extremely well. She loved the work she'd done. She'd been up late editing the photos, emailing files to Jazzy. Already this morning they'd gone back and forth in emails, and Jazzy had chosen seven of the photos she liked the best to use for her pamphlet. She was going to use others on her website. She'd told Bella when she had it updated, she'd let her know.

When Hudson had asked Bella if she minded if he dropped by to watch the shoot, she'd worried that he'd be a distraction. But he hadn't been. She'd liked having him there, sharing in the experience. His ideas were often good ones—like viewing the photos on the big-screen TV. The admiration in his eyes when he'd looked at her had almost made her tear up. She hadn't felt that kind of admiration in a very long time...if ever.

What if Hudson knew about her past? What if he knew she'd mistaken a hungry look in a teenage boy's eyes as love? What if he knew she'd gotten pregnant?

What if he knew she couldn't have children?

The statistics on her computer monitor seemed to blur for a moment. Hudson didn't need to know any of that, did he? After all, he'd said himself that he'd be leaving Rust Creek Falls. But a little voice inside her heart asked, *And what if you do get involved with him?*

The idea had been growing in momentum. It had even taken over many of her dreams. Every time she thought about the two of them together, really together, she had to struggle to push the thoughts and images away. But at night, her subconscious went wild. She woke up wanting his arms around her, needing his arms around her. But then like dreams do, they faded into reality. Her common sense prevailed, and she warned herself to keep her distance, or at least not let anything progress beyond a kiss.

However, Hudson's kisses were unforgettable.

As if she'd conjured him up by thinking about her dreams, he appeared at her desk. "I've been thinking," he said.

She gave him a smile, not knowing what was coming. "I thought I saw smoke coming from your office," she said with a straight face.

He gave her a mock scowl. "That smoke you saw was my coffeepot biting the dust. It's time I buy a single-serve brewer for in there. Any flavor you like best? I'd be willing to share."

The twinkle in his eyes told her he'd like to share

more than coffee. She shook her head. "Break room coffee is fine with me."

"Until I give you Death by Chocolate to taste," he teased. "Just you wait."

She couldn't look away from his eyes, and she didn't want to. It would be so easy to get lost in Hudson and the sparks they generated...in a fire that could consume her. She took a deep breath and slowly let it out.

"So what have you been thinking about?" she asked, getting the conversation back on track.

"I've been thinking about using your photography skills as a moneymaker for the day care center."

She tilted her head, interested.

He could obviously see that because he went on. "How would you like to take photos of moms and their babies? It would be quite a keepsake for them, plus a good promotional tool for the day care center. We can put together a child care book where we lay out the photos with parent tips. I'm sure the mothers would have plenty of those. You've seen those community cookbooks? This would be something like that. Your photos would give it that aaah factor."

"It sounds ambitious, but I'd love to participate in it."

Hudson looked thoughtful. "We could do the photos after hours, or we could commandeer the corner of one of the classrooms. Moms can stop in whenever they like, and you could make it a priority to take the photos."

"Mothers love to be photographed with their kids. I think it would be easy to convince them."

"I'd like to have it all put together by Valentine's Day," he suggested.

"That's quick."

"I know. The owner of one of the ranches I worked at self-published a history of the ranch. I helped him with it. There's a formatter I can contact. I would trust your eye on the basic layout. If we shoot the photos between Thanksgiving and New Year's, it's possible."

"I should send out an email to the parents to explain the project and encourage them to get on board. I can write something up right now and have it to you after lunch for approval."

Hudson was again pensive for a few moments. She studied his expression, the character lines on his face, the way his hair waved across his brow. Standing at her desk, he towered over her and seemed larger than life. His chest was broad, his forearms muscular beneath the rolled-up sleeves of his snap-button shirt. There was strength in those forearms, and she became distracted by the curling brown hair that covered them. Just looking at him, any part of him, sent her pulse racing.

She didn't know how long he'd been talking when his words finally broke through her thoughts. "I don't want you to go to extra work if this isn't going to fly. I'll give Walker a call or text him. After I run it by him, I'll let you know if it's a go."

"It's a wonderful idea, Hudson. It really is. You *deserve* a new coffeepot."

At that he laughed, gave her a little wave and went back to his office. Her heart was still pitter-pattering when she turned back to her computer.

Hudson was eating leftovers from a casserole Greta had prepared when Walker breezed into the day care center and his office later that day.

"That smells good," Walker said, motioning to the chicken-and-broccoli casserole that Hudson had warmed up in the microwave in the break room. "I don't imagine you made it."

"Greta made it. She doesn't let me starve."

"You settled into a good deal there. Not only horses but home cooking."

"In a way, it feels like home, more than our home ever did."

Walker gave him a surprised look. "In what way?"

"I like going there after a day here at work, or after a ride. I look forward to it."

Walker glanced around the office and the rest of the day care center. Hudson knew his brother had gone into the business because he wanted kids to have a safe, caring place to stay while their parents worked. Their own childhood with nannies who were overseeing them only because of a great salary was probably one of the reasons.

The lawsuit Walker had been involved in had also given him a new perspective. He was setting up a foundation, The Just Us Kids Pediatric Pulmonary Center, for children who need specialized medical care.

Walker returned his attention to Hudson. "So you wanted to talk to me about a scheme to make money?"

"It's not a scheme, it's a project." Hudson kept the defensiveness out of his voice. He was prepared with Bella's photos. He spread them across the desk, faced Walker and explained exactly what he had in mind.

"It would help if we could get some kind of child care expert to give quotes, too," Hudson suggested.

Walker seemed to think about all of it. "I'm surprised you came up with this."

Walker's comment irked Hudson. Yes, Walker was the CEO type, the business-oriented brother, but Hudson knew he had good ideas, too, just in a different vein.

After Walker took another look at the photos, and at the schedule Hudson had devised along with the cost estimate, his brother nodded. Then he stared at Hudson as if he were seeing him in a different way.

"I have one question," Walker said. "Will you be staying until the project is finished?"

Hudson considered his brother's question. He also considered Bella and spending more time with her. "Sure, I can stay until it's finished."

That seemed to settle everything in Walker's mind. "Go ahead," he said. "Get it started. It will be good for the day care center. It's something the other franchises could pick up and do. We could even sell it on the biggest ebook seller there is. Child care tips can be relevant to moms across the country. Quite a moneymaker you've thought up here." He extended his hand to Hudson. "Good job."

Hudson shook his brother's hand, feeling a connection with him he hadn't felt in a long time.

After Walker left, Hudson told Bella the good news. "He feels it will be a good moneymaking project and that the idea will catch on with the other franchises. He thinks we might even be able to sell it through a nationwide channel."

Bella's face was all smiles. She threw her arms around Hudson's neck and gave him a huge hug.

The impulsive gesture made him catch his breath, which only made it worse for him as he took in the scent of her perfume or shampoo or whatever smelled like flowers and Bella. He couldn't help but tighten his arms around her, and for just a few moments, she tightened her arms around him. He could feel she was breathing fast, and so was he. He wanted to bury his nose in her hair, kiss her temple and more. But she leaned away, moved her hands to his chest and looked up at him. He had to give her time. He had to give her the opportunity to come to the realization on her own that they'd be good together. One thing he was sure of—he couldn't push Bella, or she'd run. He didn't know why. He wished he did.

As if she were suddenly embarrassed, she pulled out of his arms. "I'm so happy about this. I know it's not the same as professional credits, but if I wanted to do more of this photography work, I'd have a strong recommendation."

"You might want to change what you study at college when you go back," he offered.

She looked pensive. "You might be right. On the other hand, maybe I could have a major in business administration and take photography classes, too. The best of both worlds."

Wasn't that what everybody wanted, the best of the worlds they chose? He felt as if he had one foot in an old world and one foot in a new one. He knew the old world brought him satisfaction, and he was comfortable in it. A new world? That was always a risk. But was it a risk he wanted to take?

Bella gave him a look that said she didn't know if

she should say what she was thinking, but then she seemed to make up her mind. "I couldn't help but notice you and Walker shaking hands as if you meant it."

"That's a novelty?" he joked.

"You have to get along for business's sake, I suppose. But you've never seemed...close."

"He really doesn't know what I've done on past jobs when I've worked at ranches. I guess he thinks I only wrangle calves."

"You don't talk about it?"

"Don't you know cowboys are men of few words?" Again he was teasing, but she seemed to take him seriously.

"Few words, maybe. But if they're the right words, they count."

"You and Jamie are different from me and my brothers. Maybe as kids we commiserated and told each other secrets but not as adults."

"That's a shame. But miles do make a difference. When I was at college, Jamie and I didn't talk as much or often."

"Distance can be a wedge," he agreed.

She said brightly, "But you and Walker are here now. Maybe you'll have a new start."

"Maybe," he agreed, wondering if that could be true. After all, the holidays were coming up. Weren't they the time for a new start, or a deepening of what was already there?

Bella glanced at the clock on the wall. "I told Sarah I'd help her with an art project with her class. Her aide is out this morning."

Hudson nodded. "And I have that meeting with the

pageant director, Eileen Bennet, over at the school this afternoon."

"Let me know how it goes," she said as she stepped out into the hall, giving him one of those smiles that seemed to make his heart turn sideways. He stared at her until she stepped into Sarah's classroom.

Then he looked back down at the photographs he'd printed out that were still spread across his desk. Walker had really studied them and admitted they were as great as Hudson thought they were. If Bella needed credentials to get more photography work, maybe he could help her out. He took out his cell phone and checked his contacts list. Yep, there it was. Miles Stanwick. He was the owner of a few galleries, including one in Kalispell. His headquarters, however, were in Billings. That was the great thing about cell phones. No matter where Miles was, Hudson could reach him. After two rings, Miles answered.

"Hi there, Hudson. Are you in Billings?"

"No, I'm in Rust Creek Falls. I've been taking care of business for Walker here."

"Your dad has always been one of my best clients. What can I do for you?"

"You scout out new talent, don't you?"

"I do, but I have a lot of fresh painters right now. What do you have?"

"How about photographers?"

Miles seemed to think about it. "With point-and-shoot digitals, everybody's a photographer these days. But I'm always on the lookout for something special."

"I think these photos are special, but I don't have

a gallery owner's eye. Would you consider taking a look at them?"

"I'm getting into my busy season. But sure, I can spend fifteen minutes looking over photos. Do you have my email address?"

"I do. I can send you the digital files, but I also printed them out. I think you'll see they really come to life in the glossies. I can overnight them." After Miles gave him the Billings address, he asked, "If you feel the photos have merit, do you think you'll be able to place a few?"

"If they have merit, I can always make a place for them." He paused a second, then asked, "If you're working on business for Walker, then you're not traveling much, I take it?"

"Not right now."

"Well, if you're still in Rust Creek Falls when I come over to Kalispell for the holidays, I'll give you a call. Maybe we can have dinner."

"Sounds good. And thanks, Miles. I really appreciate this."

After he ended the call, Hudson gathered up the photos. He'd email Miles the digital photos, then he'd package up the glossies and mail them on his way to the school for his meeting.

He really did think the photos were something special. He hoped Miles did, too.

He decided to keep the whole gallery query a surprise. After all, he didn't want Bella to be disappointed if nothing came of it. For now she would be happy photographing moms and babies.

An hour later, before he left for his meeting with

the pageant director, he went looking for Bella. He wanted to make sure she didn't need anything before he left. He found her in Sarah Palmer's classroom, where she was still helping with the art project, and what a project it was.

The four-year-olds were having a stupendous time with the art supplies. They were gluing and coloring without knowing they were practicing hand-eye co-ordination and fine motor skills. Sarah concentrated on that with every art project as well as burgeoning young talent. There were turkey heads and feathers cut out of construction paper, and feet, too, made of some fuzzy cord. Bella and Sarah were helping the children paste them all down on a plate that served as the turkey's body. The kids talked and laughed as they wielded crayons as if they were true artists, drawing faces on the plates.

Tommy, one of Hudson's favorites, pushed back his chair and came running over to him. "Mr. Hudson, Mr. Hudson, look at what I'm doing."

His turkey had black eyes and a mouth, and Tommy was coloring his body purple.

Hudson crouched down to Tommy's eye level. "So you've seen purple turkeys?"

Tommy looked at his turkey and the pictures of turkeys that Sarah had attached to the bulletin board.

"I didn't *see* a purple turkey," Tommy admitted. "But there could *be* purple turkeys."

At that Hudson laughed out loud. Anything was a possibility in a child's mind.

Hearing his laughter, Bella looked up. Their gazes met and Hudson could swear he felt the room shake.

But no feathers scattered, mock or otherwise, so he knew it was his imagination. Purple turkeys could give a man delusions.

The curly-headed blonde four-year-old next to Bella tapped on her arm. Hudson remembered her name was May.

"Miss Bella, I made a mistake. My line went crooked."

Hudson walked over to where Bella was seated, and he could tell the little girl's picture was supposed to resemble a house. A purple turkey. A house in a turkey's tummy. What was the difference? he supposed.

Bella rested her arm around May's shoulders. "A crooked line doesn't have to be a mistake. Let's look at what you're trying to do." She gave the plate a quarter turn. "What if we made your crooked line part of the fence that goes around the house? Sometimes they're straight and sometimes they're crooked. Your line will fit right in."

"But it can't be red. Red is for the bricks on the house," May insisted.

Bella picked up a brown crayon. "Here, give this a try on top of the red. It will make it look just like wood."

May did as Bella suggested and then looked up at her. "It does."

"You'll have a fine fence there," Hudson encouraged her. "I see you have a house with a second floor. Does it have windows on the second floor?"

No windows were showing now.

May put her finger to her lips, and then her eyes sparkled. "My house has windows. I can put in windows."

Bella said to May, "You work on that for a little while. I'll be right back." She pushed her chair away from the table and stood.

Even so, Hudson was still a head taller. For some reason, Bella made him feel ten feet tall. He wasn't sure why. Maybe it was just this "thing" between them. He felt their breathing almost synchronized as they stared at each other. He wasn't sure why that happened when he thought about kissing her, but it did.

How could he think about kissing her when they were in the middle of a room with four-year-olds?

He waved at the table and the projects spread out everywhere. "Do you think you'll ever get this cleaned up?"

"Maybe with the custodian's help," she joked. "But it's amazing how little ones like to help when you ask them. They'll pick up their scraps."

"Their feathers, you mean?" Hudson said with a straight face.

"So you got sucked into a world of purple turkeys and green feathers?"

He laughed. "It's hard to resist. Maybe that's why I like being around the kids so much. It makes the real world go away."

"Or they take you back to when you were four."

"I don't even *remember* when I was four."

"I bet if you and your brothers got together you would. No clubhouse, jungle gym, forts made out of a blanket on the sofa?"

"Are you kidding? A blanket on the sofa? Our mother would have called the maid."

Bella blinked. "I forgot."

"Forgot what?"

"You grew up very differently than I did."

What Bella meant was, he'd grown up with money. Yes, his family had been wealthy. There had been maids and housekeepers and nannies.

"Maybe I did," he said. On the other hand, though, maybe their worlds hadn't been so different after all. "But that fort you speak of...my brothers and I escaped to the woodpile now and then and rearranged it. It was a grand fort. What my mother didn't know didn't hurt her."

Bella studied him. And maybe in the atmosphere with four-year-olds around, and Sarah not too far away, she felt brave to delve into his life a bit because she asked, "How else did you escape?"

"Riding did it the most, or just wandering the pasture with the horses. How about you? How did *you* escape?"

"Books. Books took me anywhere I wanted to go, with anyone I wanted to be with. They still do. When I get the chance to settle down with one."

One of the kids dumped a canister of crayons onto the table. The scattering noise took Bella's attention for a moment. Then she asked, "Are you leaving now?"

"I am. I just wanted to remind you to call me if you need anything."

"Will do. And if I may, I'd like to remind you of something. With the pageant being held the Sunday after Thanksgiving, we don't have a lot of time to get costumes together. I'm definitely not a seamstress, and I don't know if any of the teachers are. So if we have to do any type of costumes, we need to keep it simple."

Hudson nodded. "I'll talk to Eileen about that. You should definitely sit in on the next meeting. Or maybe you should be going instead of me."

"I can go to the next one if you'd like me to. We'll have to get permission slips from parents, work up the PR for the kids being in the pageant and get that out in emails and on the website so the parents know exactly what we're doing, too."

"All good points."

Tommy waved his turkey at Hudson. Hudson went over to the four-year-old and pointed to the turkey's neck. It was still white. "Are you going to color that?"

"Maybe I'll make his neck red."

"You'll have a colorful turkey," Hudson proclaimed with a straight face.

"Maybe Miss Sarah will hang mine up high so everybody can see it."

Bella came to stand beside Hudson. "She's going to hang everyone's turkeys so when your parents come to pick you up, they'll see what a good job you did."

"And we can take them home for Thanksgiving?"

"Yes, you can."

Thanksgiving. Hudson still had no idea what he was doing for the holiday next week. He supposed Bella was planning to spend it with Jamie. Maybe in their next conversation he'd ask her. He'd spent many holidays alone, and he'd told himself he liked it that way. Memories of long-ago holidays were faded and ghostly. He almost had a hard time imagining what a real holiday would be like surrounded by family and friends he actually cared about, and who cared about him.

He should be more grateful about what he'd had growing up. After all, look at everything Bella had lost.

"Is something the matter?" she asked him.

He was going to say no, but decided to tell the truth. "I was just thinking about holidays and families and expectations that aren't usually fulfilled. Look at these kids' faces when they study their turkeys. They're totally in the present. Maybe somehow that's what we have to do to appreciate Thanksgiving and Christmas."

"When you learn how to do that, you let me know," she responded, then added, "Maybe this year the triplets will teach me their secret."

"I'm always open to hearing secrets," he said.

Bella looked startled for a moment, and then she backed away from him. "I'll see you later," she told him. "I have to get back to pasting on those feathers."

The word *secret* seemed to have spooked Bella. He supposed no one got to adulthood without a few of them.

Just what was Bella Stockton's secret?

Chapter Eight

Bella sat at her desk that afternoon, composing letters to send to parents explaining about the photos she wanted to take and the child care tips they might want to contribute. Usually moms were eager to share everything they knew about kids. She'd certainly gotten experience helping Jamie with the triplets.

Despite the work, she found herself missing Hudson. The place just wasn't the same when he wasn't there. Yes, she'd resented him when he'd first moved in, so to speak, to check up on her. But now they worked in tandem. Not only that, she missed his physical presence, the sparkle in his eyes, the energy he projected. Cowboy or businessman, he was one difficult man to ignore.

When the phone rang, she picked it up. "Just Us Kids Day Care Center, Bella Stockton speaking. How can I help you?"

"Is Hudson Jones there?" a gruff male voice asked her.

"He's not available at the moment. Can I help you?"

There was a pause. "No, I need to speak to Jones. If I leave a message, will you make sure he gets it?"

"Of course I will. Or I could put you through to his voice mail."

"I don't trust that stuff. I'd rather you hand deliver it."

She smiled and wondered how old this man was. She pulled a pink message pad and a pen from her desk. "As soon as he comes in, I'll hand it to him."

"Tell him this is Guy Boswick from Pine Bluff Ranch. He can reach me at..." And he rattled off a number. "I have a problem for him to handle."

"Can I tell him what this is in regards to?"

"No. I need to talk to him. Don't worry. He'll know who I am when you give him my name."

That was a cryptic message if she'd ever heard one. "All right, Mr. Boswick. I will do that."

"If I don't hear from him today, I'll call back tomorrow," he assured her.

"That's fine. I understand."

She hardly had the words out when Mr. Boswick said "Goodbye" and hung up.

A half hour later, Hudson blew through the door along with the wind and a few snowflakes. He had a smile on his face.

Bella couldn't help but smile back. Hudson Jones was infectious. She just hadn't figured out if that was a good thing or a bad thing.

As he took off his jacket and hung it in his office, she followed him inside, the message in her hand. "You look as if you had a good meeting."

"I did. We figured out how to keep things easy for the babies."

"I'm not sure anything is easy with babies," she warned him.

He chuckled. "Probably not. But how's this for an idea? Reindeer antler headbands for the babies, and we put them all in carriages. That way, volunteers at the school can decorate the carriages and we don't have to worry about costumes."

"I think that's brilliant," she agreed. "Did you come up with that or did Eileen?"

"A little bit of both. Eileen knows kids and what will work and what won't. I'm sure some parents must have carriages. If they don't, I'll buy a few and we'll use those."

"Is that in the budget?"

He arched his brows. "If I have to make a purchase outside the budget, we just won't tell anyone, right?"

"I don't know. Walker could mark me down for being a coconspirator."

"Not if we pull off the pageant with a big kick."

When their gazes met, Bella experienced that shaken-up feeling all over again.

Hudson hung his Stetson on the hat rack. With his flannel shirt open at the collar, dress jeans and brown boots, he was as tempting a man as she'd ever seen. But that's all he was at this point—a temptation.

She broke eye contact first, remembered the message in her hand and held it out to him. "You had an odd phone call, a Mr. Guy Boswick. He wanted me to hand deliver this to you."

Hudson took the message and studied it. "He has a problem?"

"He wouldn't tell me what it was. He just said you

knew him and you should call him back. He warned me that if you don't call him back today, he'll call again tomorrow."

"And keep calling until he gets me. That's Guy, all right."

"So you *do* know him."

"Yes, I do. I worked on his dude ranch a couple of years back. He became a father figure to me for a while. He's a tough old cowboy, but he has a good heart. I can't imagine what he wants now, though. I'd better give him a call." He looked back up at her, and she thought she could be wrong, but it seemed his eyes twinkled when he thanked her.

"Anytime," she said, meaning it.

As she went back to her desk, she realized she hadn't closed Hudson's door, nor had he. Apparently he didn't expect the conversation to be private. She liked Hudson's transparency. He said what he felt, and he meant what he said.

Bella couldn't help but overhear the beginning niceties of the conversation. After all, her desk wasn't that far away from Hudson's open door. She wasn't trying to listen, not at first. But then she heard, "You want me to accept a position in Big Timber with you at Pine Bluff? Why would I want to do that?"

He was being offered a job? Now Bella was all ears.

"I understand you have a problem you want me to solve," Hudson said. "But public perception can't be swayed easily. I have a commitment right now. Any PR firm can help you."

Bella supposed Guy Boswick was raging a powerful argument to sway Hudson to Big Timber, away from Rust Creek Falls. Maybe an emotional argument if he'd been a father figure. After all, Hudson didn't really *need* a job. He was wealthy.

"All right, I'll agree to that." Hudson listened, then asked, "How soon do you need an answer?"

Boswick must have told him and said a few more things because Hudson ended with, "It was good talking with you again, too, Guy. Take care," and he set down the cordless phone.

Hudson looked Bella's way, and she couldn't pretend she hadn't heard. Rising from her desk, she went into his office. "Maybe I'm sorry I gave you that message. I couldn't help but overhear. Did he offer you a job?"

"Yes, he did. But I don't know all the details yet. Someone from the ranch is going to be contacting me. Then I'll know more."

"When would it start?" she asked hesitantly.

"Bella, there's really nothing to talk about. Everything's supposition at this point."

"But when we talked about putting together the child care book, I was under the impression you were going to stay until Valentine's Day, right?"

"I don't want to talk about this now, Bella. I have a lot to think about and information to get. I *will* tell you I'll be out for a couple of hours tomorrow. Actually, maybe I'll just take the whole day. I need to clear my head, go riding, maybe work some colts. That will probably be the best thing for everyone. If you need me, you can reach me on my cell."

Bella decided not to mope. She'd known what kind of man Hudson was when he'd arrived. He'd told her point-blank he was a traveling man and not one to remain in one place. So she certainly hadn't been weaving dreams about him staying, had she? Valentine's Day or sooner, he was going to be leaving again, and she'd better get used to the idea.

She raised her chin when she replied, "I won't need you, Hudson. I managed Just Us Kids just fine before you got here. I can certainly handle it tomorrow."

As she turned to leave his office, he called her back. "Bella?"

She stopped but kept her shoulders squared and her back rigid, her head held high.

"Life is about choices, and they happen every day. This is just another one of those choices."

"Commitments happen every day, too," she returned, then went to her desk and ignored Hudson for the rest of the day.

The atmosphere between Bella and Hudson remained excruciatingly strained after his phone call to Guy Boswick. This was one time when she had no idea what he was thinking. Could he seriously be considering taking a job in Big Timber? Riding the range again? Training horses? He was a man of many talents, that was for sure.

As she worked at her desk all day on Thursday, she couldn't stop herself from wondering where he was and what he was doing. Couldn't stop herself from missing him. It was odd when you got used to a person's presence. When the individual was gone, a piece of your heart was, too. No, not her heart, she told herself. She couldn't care that much about Hudson. Could she?

She thought about the days and weeks and months

after she and Jamie had been split up from their other siblings. Each minute at first, and then each hour, and finally each day, she'd wondered where they were and what they were doing. She and Jamie had been too young and hadn't had the means to keep track of them. Their grandparents had made it clear their sisters and brothers were no longer their concern. Were Liza, Dana, Bailey, Daniel and Luke bitter and resentful? Was that why they never called or returned...because Rust Creek Falls had nothing but bad memories of the split-up after their parents' deaths? And sadness. All good reasons not to return, she supposed.

The day rolled along even though Bella didn't put much gusto into it. At least not until she visited the classrooms to talk and play with the kids. But when she returned to her desk, she fell into the same thoughts, missing Hudson and wondering if he was actually considering the job offer. Knowing she could only make herself crazy, she forced herself to stop. Her life certainly didn't revolve around his, and his would never revolve around hers. At least not with any permanence.

Could an affair assuage some of what she felt for Hudson? Or was it already too late for that? He could even be gone before Christmas.

In an effort to get her mind off him, she returned to her year-end report. She didn't pick her head up until one of the moms, the one who had threatened to take her son to another day care center if she saw evidence of a sniffle, entered Just Us Kids to pick up Jimmy. Marla Tillotson never seemed to be happy. Bella had glimpsed a smile on her face once in a while when she was with her son, but not often. Bella had also noticed that Marla stirred up gossip with the other moms. She managed a new laundromat that had opened up recently, so she was in contact with many town residents. When she heard news, she spread it around.

As Marla approached the desk, Bella pulled out the clipboard with the sign-out sheets. She handed it to her with a smile and asked politely, "Is it getting any colder out there?"

"Cold enough to trade leather boots for fur-lined ones," Marla said. Her gaze went to Hudson's office. "So Mr. Jones took the whole day off?" she asked. "I noticed he wasn't here this morning either."

Bella wouldn't gossip, but she would be honest. "Mr. Jones took a personal day today."

Marla gave her a wicked smile. "I'll say it was personal."

Bella couldn't keep her eyebrows from arching up. "Excuse me?" she asked, knowing she shouldn't pursue it, yet interested in most anything about Hudson.

"I stopped in at the Ace in the Hole for takeout for lunch. He was there with a very beautiful redhead. They seemed to know each other well, at least from the way he was patting her hand. They didn't seem in any hurry to eat and were enjoying glasses of wine."

Bella felt as if she'd been stabbed. Hudson had taken off today for a date? A long lunch with afternoon delight afterward?

Should she be surprised?

With Hudson's charming nature, he'd been in Rust Creek Falls long enough to make friendships, to meet lots of women. She turned back to Marla. "Mr. Jones's business is his alone," she said, her voice devoid of inflection. "Go ahead back to Jimmy's classroom. I'm sure he'll be ready to leave."

Marla gave Bella an odd look, then a little shrug. She went down the hall to her son's classroom.

Bella was not going to give another thought to Hudson Jones.

Not one more thought.

When Hudson came to work the next morning, he looked somber as he gave Bella a nod then went to his office. He didn't say good-morning. He didn't ask how the day had gone yesterday. In essence, he was quieter than she'd ever seen him, and he stayed that way.

Was it because of the kisses they'd shared that she now felt piqued that he was ignoring her? Was it because of their argument? The possibility he'd be leaving?

As the day progressed, and he stayed in his office on his computer, she imagined exactly what he'd been doing yesterday. Maybe he was so quiet because he'd had a marvelous afternoon and evening in bed with the redhead. Maybe the redhead had turned his head. Maybe...

Maybe too many things. She was tired of her mind running in circles or supposition playing havoc with her thoughts. Maybe they should just get everything out on the table and then worry about digesting it.

The afternoon seemed tediously slow as she thought about what she could say, what she could ask. Eventually she signed out the last parent and child, and she watched all the teachers leave.

That left her and Hudson. Now was the time.

He was still at his computer, studying the screen as if it held the answers to the universe, when she marched into his office.

He swiveled away from the monitor and gave his attention to her. "Are you leaving?"

"In a minute. First I have something to ask you."

"Go ahead."

"Why did you ignore me all day? Because I'd like to know whether you're keeping your commitment to Just Us Kids or not."

"I didn't ignore you today."

"I don't know what you'd call it. You hardly said two words."

"I have a lot on my mind. My mood had nothing to do with you."

For some reason that conclusion annoyed her more than anything else. It seemed she was becoming of no importance to him. Or was it that he had become too important to her?

Because she wasn't used to caring for a man, because she had too many thoughts spinning around in her head, she blurted out, "Oh, I understand it had nothing to do with me. That's probably because you must have had a spectacular time yesterday with the redhead."

After his brows arched and he leaned back in his desk chair, she realized Hudson looked totally surprised at her outburst. Meeting her gaze directly, he said, "Lunch with that redhead was all about business. Period."

Bella felt a red flush begin at her neck and start to creep up into her cheeks. She felt like an absolute fool, and she couldn't stand here and face Hudson another second. In one continuous motion she left his office, grabbed her coat that she'd laid over her desk chair, as well as her purse from the bottom drawer, and made for the door.

By that time, Hudson was standing in the doorway to his office. "Bella—"

But she couldn't look at him right now. She couldn't talk to him reasonably, not after she'd acted like a foolish teenager, the foolish teenager she'd once been. She rushed out of the day care center and into her car, then pulled away in a burst of speed.

Hudson had two reactions to Bella's sudden departure. The first—he was worried about her. But the second... Was that jealousy he'd detected? If she was jealous, did that mean she cared about him a bit?

He could go after her, but he expected she needed time to calm down, time to realize they were going to have to talk about this eventually. As he walked through the rooms, closing up the place, he realized he'd been wrong when he'd said his mood today had had nothing to do with her. It had actually had a lot to do with her. Yes, their argument. But more than that, everything else that was on his mind, too.

The woman Guy had sent to meet with him was basically his ranch manager; she took care of the books, scheduling, vet appointments, and kept all running smoothly. She had been a looker, that was true. And in the past, Hudson had wanted to look.

This time he didn't.

He hadn't cared at all what she looked like. But he'd

listened to what she'd said, and that had caused him more turmoil. He tried to decide whether he should stay or leave Rust Creek Falls. Point one, did Just Us Kids still need him? The day care center was back on track now, the client base saved, rumors put to rest, the scare of another epidemic almost resolved. Was there a need for him to stay?

He'd told Walker he'd stay until the book project was completed. No, it hadn't been a hard-and-fast promise, but he did always keep his word. Besides, he'd found he actually liked living in Rust Creek Falls, especially at Clive's ranch. But there was one more reason compelling him to stay. And her name was Bella.

Bella drove home, her face still flushed from her encounter with Hudson and her own stupidity. She usually filtered what came out of her mouth. What had happened?

At the ranch house, she jumped out of her car and practically ran inside. This ranch had become a safe haven. But as she stepped over the threshold, she realized it might be safe, but it was noisy, too.

The babies were squalling for their dinner, and Jamie just shook his head. "Paige couldn't come tonight, so I said I could handle them on my own."

She could see that he was trying to, but more than anything, she could see how exhausted her brother was. Slipping out of her coat, she hurried to help him feed the triplets. With two of them catching spills, wiping sticky hands and playing airplane games, they soon had the babies fed. Bathing, however, took a little longer.

By the time they'd settled all three in their cribs and returned downstairs, Jamie looked at Bella with a weak smile. "You didn't get anything to eat."

"I'm not hungry," she said honestly, still remembering what had happened with Hudson. How was she going to live that down?

Her brother's shoulders slumped a bit as he picked up dirty dishes from the table and took them to the sink. She could tell he was practically dead on his feet, and she knew he needed more than a good night's sleep. He needed a break.

She pulled out a kitchen chair and pointed to it. "Sit."

"I have to clean up the kitchen," he reminded her.

"No, you don't. I'll do it. I want to talk to you."

"That sounds ominous," he said as he sat in the chair, obviously too fatigued to argue with her.

"You have to take a break from everything or you're going to collapse." When he started to protest, she held up her hand. "I'm going to ask for Monday off. I want you to call a motel in Kalispell and leave tomorrow morning for a few days. I want you to get some rest while I take charge of the babies and the schedule and the ranch chores."

"You can't do it on your own."

"You're going to have to trust me, Jamie. The baby chain will help with the triplets, and if I need help with the chores I can call our neighbor's son." When he began to protest again, she cut him off. "You're not going to be any good to the triplets or the ranch if you fall over from exhaustion or get sick. You probably haven't had a solid night's sleep since they were born."

"Since they came home," he admitted. "I think I hear them, and I wake up to check, or I worry that I'm not going to hear them."

"Or one of them cries," Bella added. "Believe me, I understand. That's why you have to do this. You have to depend on me as I've always depended on you."

"What about you?" he asked.

"I've actually *had* breaks—like that afternoon I went riding." Like the afternoon she'd slept on Hudson's couch. "I even get a break at work," she added.

"Around all those kids?"

"I don't have direct responsibility for them—the teachers do. I can take my lunch break without worrying or take a walk."

Or stop in Hudson's office to talk to him, she thought. But that wasn't going to happen again.

Jamie got quiet. He actually seemed to be considering her offer. Finally he looked at her and said, "I'll only do this if the neighbor boy can come over and help you with the chores."

"Call him and the motel. Any motel you want."

"Just something with a bed would be good," he admitted.

"I'll call Hudson and ask him about Monday." She hoped she'd just get his voice mail.

But that, of course, didn't happen. He answered his cell on the second ring. But before he could say anything, she launched into an explanation.

After a moment's hesitation, Hudson assured her, "No problem. Take the day off. I can cover for you."

"Great," she said, ready to hang up.

"Bella, about this afternoon…"

"I really have to go, Hudson. I think I hear one of the triplets. I'll see you Tuesday."

And before he could say more, she ended the call.

Was it the cowardly way out? Possibly, but she was also buying time. Maybe in a couple of days he'd forget about her outburst. Simply put, it might not have been that important to him. If it wasn't, she was off the hook.

If it was…she'd deal with Hudson on Tuesday.

Chapter Nine

Hudson knew the longer a misunderstanding went unattended, the more mucked up life could get. That's why he decided to visit Bella on Sunday. He knew a phone call wouldn't do it. If she was taking care of the triplets with Jamie gone, she'd be too busy to focus on a call. Besides, this explanation required face-to-face time. He had a feeling she didn't believe him about his lunch with the redhead being purely business.

Considering the fact she thought he was the love-'em-and-leave-'em type, it was very possible. Love them and leave them. Yep, that's what he'd done in the past. It was easier than getting involved and getting hurt. He'd always made that clear at the outset with whomever he dated. But Bella?

She seemed to turn his world and his perceptions of it upside down.

When he arrived at Jamie's house and stood on the porch outside the door, he still wasn't sure what he was going to say. He did realize, however, that there wasn't another vehicle in the driveway. That was odd since the baby chain always helped on weekends as well as during the week. Hudson was aware of the sound of squalling babies from inside. Two of them, if he could make out the sounds. He rang the doorbell and heard Bella's voice.

"Oh my gosh, Paige, I'm so glad you could make it after all."

Then she opened the door and saw Hudson.

The baby in Bella's arms was squirming and squiggling and obviously wanted to be let down. He was squalling as loud as his little lungs would allow.

"Which one is this?" Hudson yelled above the din.

Though obviously surprised at his presence, Bella answered reflexively, "Henry."

More crying came from inside the living room. Looking past Bella, Hudson could see a baby dressed all in pink, so he supposed it was Katie, wailing with the best of them. She was seated in a play saucer, but that definitely wasn't occupying her.

He reached out and said, "Give me Henry. You go take care of Katie."

Bella didn't seem sure she wanted to give up the little boy, so Hudson took matters into his own hands. He reached for Henry with a big smile. "Come on, fella. You and I have to talk."

The baby reached his arms out to Hudson, and Hudson took him, raising the baby's face to his own. "You'll get ahead in life better if you don't scream so much. Come on, let's figure out what's wrong."

Hudson walked Henry into the living room and saw the third triplet, Jared, sitting in a playpen playing with blocks. The only cooperative one in the bunch.

Henry had obviously been surprised by Hudson lifting him and talking to him. His cries subsided into hiccups until Hudson settled him into the crook of his arm. Then Henry started all over again.

Puzzled, Hudson jiggled him a bit. "What? Wet diaper? Hungry? Bored? You'll have to tell me."

Henry stopped crying as if he was considering it, and Hudson stuck his finger into the boy's diaper. "He's wet," he called to Bella. "Where are the diapers?"

Bella motioned to a changing table on the other side of the room, and Hudson went that way. He'd learned a thing or two working at the day care center. There, one had to be a man of all trades, so to speak. He not only learned how to change diapers, but also how to give belly rubs and tickle toes. Anything to get a baby to do what you wanted him to do.

Grabbing hold of a rubber ducky on the changing table, he laid Henry down and handed it to him. "You play with this while we take care of business."

By this time Bella had taken Katie out of the play saucer. The little girl had stopped crying as soon as Bella lifted her into her arms.

Now that Henry was concentrating on the rubber ducky, and Katie was quiet, Bella asked Hudson, "What are you doing here?"

"We need to talk." He unsnapped Henry's jeans and took off the wet diaper. "But more important, why don't you have any help today?"

"Fallon caught a flu bug she didn't want to give to the babies. Paige and the others couldn't cover because of church functions or holiday gatherings. Paige said she'd get here as soon as she could."

Hudson fumbled a bit with the dry diaper. He wasn't as adept at it as Bella or the teachers and aides at the day care center. The sticky tab caught on his thumb, bent over and stuck to itself. But somehow he managed to diaper Henry, even if it was a little lopsided.

"I was going to give them a snack," Bella said. "Maybe we can talk if we can get them all eating a cookie at the same time."

"Sounds good," Hudson agreed, snapping Henry's jeans and pulling down his little shirt. When he hefted Henry into his arms, the little boy gave him what Hudson thought was a smile. Hudson felt as if he'd accomplished something big.

After he carried Henry into the kitchen and settled him into a high chair, Bella did the same with Katie. Then she hurried back into the living room to gather up Jared. Soon the triplets were gnawing on cookies.

Bella turned to him. "Would you like something to drink? Soda, milk, juice?"

"Milk would be fine. I'm still a growing boy."

Bella shook her head and gave him a small smile as she went to the refrigerator, poured two glasses of milk and set them on the table.

Hudson was thinking about the best way to start when she plunged in first. "I'm sorry I reacted as I did on Friday. I had no right."

Hudson decided to ignore her remark about her rights. Instead, he said, "Tell me why you reacted as you did."

"Because of what Marla Tillotson said."

After she finished explaining, Hudson pressed,

"And why did that bother you so much? That I might have been having lunch with a redhead."

Bella suddenly gave all her attention to Katie, wiping a few crumbs from her cheek. "Hudson..."

"All right, I'll let that go for now. But let me explain the whole situation to you. Guy sent his ranch manager—who just happens to be a pretty redhead—to convince me he needs me in Big Timber. Apparently he thought she could do a better job at it than he could."

"Because you like pretty redheads?" Bella asked seriously.

Hudson knew a little honesty might go a long way with Bella. "In the past, I've been known to have my head turned by a pretty woman. Guy witnessed that."

"Why does he think you're the right person for this job? Exactly what is it?" Bella asked, moving away from the topic.

"Last season, one of the ranch's patrons had an accident. Guy took an economic hit over it. He had clients cancel their reservations. They're trying to get past it. They've seen how I turned around the reputation of Just Us Kids, and they want me to do that for them."

"Are you going to take the job?"

Hudson couldn't tell from Bella's voice or her expression whether she cared personally or professionally.

He said honestly, "I don't know. Just Us Kids really doesn't need me any longer. Guy is a friend. But any PR firm could help him."

Before she could respond, Bella's phone emitted a lively ringtone. Hesitating only a second, she took it from her shirt pocket and studied the screen. "It's Jamie. I need to take this. Excuse me."

He gave her a wink. "I'll watch this tribe while you talk."

She answered the call. "Hi, Jamie... Everything's fine... I told you, you don't need to check every few hours."

Even though Jamie was taking a break, Hudson realized he still had the triplets and Bella on his mind. Of course he'd be checking in often.

"We're good. Order room service. Eat a lot. Sleep, and watch mindless TV. That's an order."

Her brother said something that made her laugh. "Yes, that is a change, isn't it? Really, we're good. And I don't want to hear from you again until you come home tomorrow night. Fine. I'll text you after they're all settled in for the night. And I'll give them extra kisses from you. See you tomorrow."

Ending the call, she pocketed the phone once more.

"I admire your loyalty to your brother," he said sincerely.

Bella went to the refrigerator and pulled out a casserole dish. She showed it to Hudson. "Cherry cobbler. Our volunteers bring casseroles and desserts when they come. Would you like some?"

"Sure," Hudson agreed. "That will go great with milk."

Efficiently Bella microwaved two dishes of cobbler and brought them to the table. She sat across from him, the babies between them.

Despite everything, Hudson felt a connection to Bella, a connection that was growing stronger. Just now, when she'd offered him this snack, it was as if she'd made a decision of sorts, and he wondered what was coming.

She stirred her cobbler a bit, forgot about her spoon and looked him straight in the eyes. "Jamie and I have been a team for years."

"Anyone can see that," Hudson commented, lost in her face, the point of her chin, the tilt of her cheek bones, the brown of her eyes.

"We became a team for a reason."

"Your parents died. That brought you closer together," Hudson said. She'd already told him that.

"That wasn't the only reason we became a team. We have five other siblings—Luke, Daniel, Dana, Bailey and Liza."

Hudson was stunned. He didn't know what to say. But then he remarked, "No one in town mentioned it."

"Anyone who knows us respects what we've been through. They know we've had a lot of heartache, and some of that is due to not having any contact with our other siblings."

"Why not?"

"After our parents' accident, we were split apart. Dana and Liza were sent away and adopted because they were younger. Our grandparents considered me and Jamie too young to be involved, and they didn't tell us much about it. Luke, Daniel and Bailey were over eighteen and considered adults. Our grandparents said they couldn't handle more mouths to feed, so the three boys left town. They were just as traumatized by our parents' deaths even though they were older. On top of that, I think they were bitter and resentful that my grandparents essentially kicked them out on their own."

"Have you tried contacting them?"

"I've tried. Not directly, of course, because I don't know where any of them are. But I've used search engines. I haven't had any luck."

"And none of them have ever contacted you?"

Hudson could see the anguish on Bella's face as she shook her head. "It hurts," she said. "Jamie has never left Rust Creek Falls, and I've been here except for college. It would be easy to find us. But apparently they don't want to. That's why Jamie and I have been as close as we are."

Finally Hudson thought he understood the depth of Bella's loneliness. As much as he and his brothers squabbled, they stayed connected. Reaching out, he covered her hand with his. "I'm sorry for all you've lost."

"I don't need anyone's pity," she said quietly. "That's why Jamie and I don't talk about it."

"Thank you for confiding in me. That means you trust me."

Bella looked as if she might say more, but then she pushed her chair back and stood. "Maybe we can settle this crew down for a nap. Getting them all quiet and sleeping at the same time could be an impossible feat, but we can try. That is, if you can stay. If you can't, I understand."

Hudson wasn't going anywhere, not until he was sure Bella could handle what she'd taken on.

Although they worked together at the day care center, Bella was surprised to find they also seemed to work well around the babies in the kitchen. She couldn't help sneaking peeks at Hudson as he wiped Henry's mouth or as he plucked a piece of cookie from Katie's hair. He was big and tall, but he was gentle and caring. He was almost as good around the babies as Jamie was.

When he'd thanked her for trusting him, she'd almost told him about her pregnancy and the baby she'd miscarried. She almost told him that she loved taking care of Jamie's babies because she might never have any of her own. Watching Hudson with Katie and Jared and Henry, she could easily see he'd want kids of his own someday.

She thought again about the job offer he'd received. Another good reason not to confide in him. There was no point. Whether she trusted him or not, whether he was attracted to her or not, he was most likely going to be leaving again. Rust Creek Falls was just a stopover in his nomadic lifestyle.

To her surprise, Henry was the baby who quieted first. After they laid him in his crib, he stuck his thumb in his mouth, and his eyes soon closed. It took longer for Katie and Jared. She and Hudson walked them and rocked them until finally they both dozed off. After settling them in their cribs, Bella gave Hudson a smile as they left the room and went downstairs.

In the living room, she made sure the monitor was turned on. "They could wake up in five minutes," she told Hudson.

"Or they could give you a break for at least a half hour or maybe longer."

"Do you always see the world in positive terms?" she asked.

"I try to. But then most of my life has been pretty positive. My family might not be all I want it to be, but I have one. I've never had to think about money. I can pretty much go where I want to go and do what I want. I'm grateful for all that. Every day at the day care center I see single moms struggling and dads working two jobs. I look at folks who were hit by the flood here and what they've lost. I can't help but be grateful for what I have."

"I like your outlook," Bella said.

He stepped closer to her. "Is that all you like?"

She tried to keep the moment light. "I could make a list," she teased.

"And I could make a list of everything I like about you. It would be a long one."

He was right there now, close to her. He loomed over her, but she didn't feel intimidated. In fact, everything about Hudson being near her excited her. Feelings surged through her that almost made her reach for him. When she thought about that redhead, she hated the idea of Hudson kissing another woman, holding another woman, making love to another woman. Bella wanted to *be* that woman.

He must have seen the hunger in her eyes because he took her into his arms and kissed her. His lips were unerringly masculine, supremely masterful, absolutely intoxicating. His arms held her a little tighter, and she pressed closer. His scent, man and aftershave, was intoxicating. He was so ultimately sexy. As they kissed, her hand came up to his cheek, and her fingers trailed over beard stubble. When he groaned, she felt as if she'd accomplished a monumental feat.

As if he wanted to accomplish that same feat, he laced his fingers in her hair. He swept his tongue through her mouth until she had no breath left for anything but Hudson. They kept tasting each other as if they could never get enough and gave in to desire that they'd denied for weeks. He backed her up, and she knew what was behind them—the sofa. She didn't protest or even think about refusing. Her head might know better, but her heart wanted Hudson...wanted him in a primal way.

They'd almost reached their destination...

Then the doorbell rang.

It took a few moments for Bella to realize some-one was at the door. She tore away from Hudson, her head spinning, her mouth throbbing from his kiss, her senses filled with him.

"I have to get that," she murmured. "It could be... anyone."

No, she definitely couldn't think straight. That was for sure.

Hudson's eyes held a glazed look, too, and she won-dered if he'd been as into that kiss as she had been. Was that even possible? Had she lost her mind? She'd just listed all the reasons she shouldn't confide in him and couldn't get involved with him.

Then what had she done?

She'd kissed him.

To her dismay, that hadn't been an ordinary kiss. That had been a lead-to-something-else kiss.

The doorbell rang again, and she practically ran to

the foyer and pulled open the door. She was so glad to see Paige's face.

But Paige took one look at Bella and asked, "Is something wrong?"

"Oh, no. No," Bella assured her, pulling her inside. "I thought you couldn't get here this soon."

"Our meeting ended earlier than I thought it would. How are you coping?"

"Oh, I'm coping just fine. In fact, Hudson's here. He helped me put the triplets to bed. Believe it or not, they're actually all napping."

Paige was giving her an are-you-sure-I'm-not-interrupting-something look.

But Bella kept shaking her head. "Come on in. I can use your help. Jamie called, and I convinced him I had everything under control." She prattled on, filling the air with chitchat, which was so unlike her.

Paige knew that, and Hudson did, too. But she had to do something to cover up that kiss, to process it, to absorb the way she felt when Hudson kissed her.

By the time she and Paige were inside the living room, Hudson had seemed to compose himself, too. He'd taken his Stetson off the table where he'd laid it when he'd come in and plopped it onto his head.

To Bella he said, "It looks as if you have reinforcements, so I'll be on my way. Nice to see you, Paige."

"Good to see you, too, Hudson."

There was an awkward silence until Bella offered, "I'll walk you out. Paige, I'll be right back. The monitor's on."

It would have been easier and less awkward if Bella had just let Hudson leave. But she'd just have to face him when she returned to work if she didn't deal with their kiss now.

He stepped out onto the porch and then turned to look at her. They were eye level. "It seemed right," he simply said, and she knew what he meant. Everything about that kiss had seemed right.

"Maybe, but I'm glad Paige interrupted. We both need time to think."

He shook his head. "Maybe we should stop thinking and just feel."

"Hudson, there's still a lot you don't know about me."

"So tell me."

If she did that, she'd be plunging into the unknown. If she did that, she'd be asking for rejection. Impulsively, she leaned forward and gave Hudson a light kiss on the lips.

"I'll see you at work on Tuesday morning," she said.

He looked as if he wanted to take her into his arms again, but she backed up, and he seemed to understand. He nodded. "See you Tuesday morning."

When Bella closed the door, she couldn't help but imagine exactly what would have happened if Paige hadn't arrived.

Hudson was out of sorts. When he arrived back at the Lazy B, he went straight to the barn. After a stop at the tack room, he saddled up Breeze, mounted and took a path through the fields where the snow had melted. He needed a horse under him, the wind in his face, the cold against his skin.

As he rode, he realized he just hadn't been able to

go into the empty ranch house. The reason? He wanted Bella there with him. He wasn't sure yet what all that entailed, but he knew he wanted to make a few of his dreams come true—the ones that included Bella in his bed. If they hadn't been interrupted this afternoon, they would have had sex on that couch. The thing was, if Paige hadn't interrupted them, one of the babies might have. That would have been even more awkward.

When he made love to Bella, he wanted no interruptions and no one interfering. He wanted their attention to be focused on just the two of them. He also wanted Bella to be sure…to want him as much as he wanted her. To his surprise, that wasn't just about lust. It wasn't just about the fun they could have in the sheets, the satisfaction of two bodies coming together. No, these feelings went deeper. He felt protective toward Bella. He didn't want her to be confused or unsure. Most of all, he didn't want to hurt her. If they shared a bed, they'd both have to do it freely. Consequences and the future be damned.

The problem was, he'd never felt protective like this about a woman before. He'd never cared about her dreams, her insecurities, her past. He cared about all of that with Bella. She'd lost her parents, her brothers and sisters. He could understand why she wouldn't want to willingly lose any more.

He didn't want to lose anything either…especially not his freedom. He felt vulnerable and didn't like that at all. He didn't like the idea that a woman could cause upset or joy or create a hunger he just had to satisfy.

Bella confused him. That was a first, and he'd like it to be a last.

He had no idea what he was going to do about any of it.

Chapter Ten

Hudson could fry himself a burger. He could even flip an omelet. What he couldn't usually do was bake. But he'd missed Bella at Just Us Kids, as did everyone else, and he wanted to bake something to welcome her back on Tuesday. She did so much for the teachers, the parents and especially the children, making them feel comforted and loved. In essence, she was the poster girl for Just Us Kids. More than that, she was the heart.

At first he hadn't known what to do that would be special yet not over-the-top. He'd nixed flowers right away. Spending tons of money on every rare flower there was and filling her desk with them was too showy and too impersonal. Besides, he wanted to show her another side of him—one that could be caring in ways that counted rather than only spending money.

After consulting a clerk at the grocery store, he found a box of what she said were never-fail cupcakes. He had to do cupcakes, of course, so they could pass them out and share them with the kids. She showed him the muffin pans to buy and colorful little cups. After one look at him, and hearing his woe that he'd never made icing in his life, let alone a cake, she showed him canned icing. That would have to do.

Before he took all his supplies to the checkout, she asked, "Why don't you just buy cupcakes or a cake from the bakery? We'd decorate it really nice and even put her name on it."

But Hudson just shook his head. "That's not the same thing at all. I don't want to buy the cupcakes. I want to make them for her."

The woman gave him a wink and a nod as if she understood, and Hudson left with his purchases, full of hope.

Actually the baking went fairly well, except for a few spills when he poured the batter. The icing, however, was something different. When he realized he'd bought only white and pink, he decided to swirl it and get a little fancy with it. White with a pink swirl, pink with a white swirl. At the end of his project, he had to admit he would never be a cake decorator. But the cupcakes looked presentable, and that's what mattered.

He left early for the day care center, in plenty of time to hang the pink-and-white crepe paper the store clerk had told him would be a good decoration. He wanted everything ready before anyone else arrived.

And he was ready. As the teachers filed in, he was glad Bella wasn't among them. He wanted as many teachers and kids here as possible before she came through that door.

All of the teachers were there and some of the children, too, when she came in, saw the decorations and the big sign that said Welcome Back, Bella. Her mouth dropped open.

Her gaze went to Sarah, but Sarah just shrugged. "Not our doing." She pointed to Hudson.

One of the other teachers, Joyce Croswell, pointed to the cupcakes. "And just look at those. He made them, too." Her gaze went from Bella to Hudson, as if everyone should realize something more was going on than boss and day care center manager.

Bella looked absolutely paralyzed for a moment, but then she recovered and smiled. "I don't know what to say." She went over to Hudson, threw her arms around him and gave him a huge hug. "No one's ever done anything like this for me before. And I was only gone one day."

"Bella Stockton," he said seriously, loud enough for everyone to hear, "you make this place go round. We all felt the length of the day you were gone because you weren't here to experience it with us. We missed your smile and your energy and your caring, and we just wanted to let you know."

Bella looked close to tears now, and he hadn't wanted that. "Come on," he said. "Taste one of the cupcakes, then everyone else can have one, too. I made enough to go around." He took one of the paper plates they used for snacks with the kids and placed one of the pink cupcakes on it. Then he handed it to her. She studied the cupcake with its little white swirl on the top.

They were standing quite close together now, and she murmured again, "I can't believe you went to all this trouble."

"No trouble, Bella, not for you. Not to show you that I think about you and I care about you." He didn't think anyone else had heard what he'd just said, but he could see in Bella's eyes that she had.

"Aw, Hudson."

The door flew open, and two moms and their babies came in. Their special moment was gone.

"I'd better wait to eat this until I can really enjoy it," Bella told him.

"Lunchtime?" he asked.

"Sure, if no crisis erupts. But at least I can taste the icing." Taking her finger, she swiped at the white point on top of the cupcake. He watched her as she slowly placed it on her lip. Her tongue came out, licking the confection, and she closed her eyes and smiled. "It's sweet, Hudson, just like icing should be."

"It came from a can," he said, now wishing he had tried to make it himself.

"It's the thought that counts. It's pretty and it tastes good, and it's perfect on the cupcakes. I'll have a lot more than that little taste at lunchtime. I promise."

Rattled by the sheer sensuality of watching her lick that icing with her tongue, he almost broke into a sweat. Composing himself, he took trays of cupcakes to each classroom and passed them out to the children who were old enough to have them. The others he took to the break room, protecting them with a plastic covering. Then he waited for lunchtime.

Bella had seen that look in Hudson's eyes—the one that excited her. She was never so happy it was finally lunchtime. When she went to the break room, he was already there. Apparently Greta had made him some kind of casserole he could warm up in the microwave.

He had the flowered dish in front of him, and he was forking pasta with ground beef into his mouth.

He stopped when she brought her bagged lunch and a paper plate to the table. "If you'd like something hot, I'll share. There's plenty here."

"I'm fine with this." She nodded at her turkey sandwich. But as she ate it, the smell of the casserole made her mouth water. He must have seen her eyeing it because he took her paper plate and forked some of the casserole onto it. Then he gave her another fork that had been sitting beside his dish.

"Did you expect company?" she asked.

"Sure did. I want to make sure you enjoy your cupcake." And before the electricity zipping between them got a little too hot, he asked, "How's Jamie?"

"He looks better, and he seems rested. I think the time away did him good."

"And you survived," he said with respect in his voice.

"I did...with help. Including yours."

His visit to the ranch house brought to mind that kiss. That kiss she'd never forget.

After that, they made small talk about the day care center while they ate. When they'd both finished, Hudson rose, chose two cupcakes from the tray and brought one over to Bella.

"Coffee with that?" he asked.

"Sure." She'd never had a man serve her cupcakes and coffee before. This was truly a first.

He took milk from the refrigerator and poured just the amount she liked into her mug, then set it on the table. He poured a black coffee for himself.

Trying to be ladylike, she took the paper from the cupcake and then used her fork to take one bite, and then another. "These are really good. Maybe you can give Greta a run for her money in the baking department."

He ate his cupcake in three bites, then responded, "I doubt that. This was just a lucky first try. Or maybe I just had good motivation."

Her fork stopped halfway to her mouth. They gazed at each other, and Bella's heart beat so fast she could hardly swallow.

He leaned forward and with his forefinger touched the top of her lip. "You have some icing there," he said. His touch held fire, and she couldn't help wishing it was his lips that were meeting hers.

"I'd kiss you again," he said, as if reading her thoughts, "but that wouldn't be proper at the workplace."

With Hudson looking at her with those bedroom eyes of his, proper didn't seem to have a place in her world. Should she be fighting this attraction? What if she just gave in to it and enjoyed it? Enjoyed herself with a man? Maybe for the first time ever.

"I should get back to my desk," she murmured, to put that very temptation out of her mind.

But before she could rise to her feet, Hudson covered her hand with his. "Look, I don't know what you've heard about me or my reputation, but I don't just go around kissing random women."

She didn't know what to say to that, so she waited for Hudson to go on.

He cleared his throat, as if putting his feelings into

words was hard for him. "You're such a pretty woman. I'm sure lots of men want to kiss you."

Considering her history and her situation, nothing could be further from the truth. Most of the men in town now considered her standoffish. That was ironic considering her wild teenage years when she was anything but. She couldn't help but laugh wryly at his comment.

But when she did, Hudson leaned away, took his hand from hers and seemed to be insulted. She knew he was when he asked, "Do you consider my kissing you amusing, or our kisses just a joke?"

Anything but. He actually looked a bit vulnerable, and she wondered if she'd hurt him. Could he really care about her?

"I'm just botching this and making a fool of myself," he said, standing.

But before he could stride out of the room, she hopped to her feet and caught his arm. "I didn't mean to laugh, but you don't know—"

"I know how much I'm attracted to you. Are you attracted to me?"

She gave a small nod, and suddenly she was in his arms and he was kissing her again. It was a short kiss, though a deep, wet one.

He set her away from him. "I know you're worried about your job. Considering what happened with my brother and Lindsay, I understand your concern. Believe me. But there are no repercussions with what's going on with us here. You can walk away, and your job will still be safe. I've wanted you for weeks, but I

understand that you're young, and I'll back off if that's
what you want."

She was deeply touched by everything he'd said
because she could see he meant it all. She could also
see something else. Because she was young, he could
possibly believe she was a virgin, that she was inex-
perienced. She had to be honest with him and set him
straight.

"Hudson, this isn't my first rodeo."

He looked a bit surprised at her comment, so she
went on. "You've been on my mind for weeks, too. I
have so many decisions to make in my life. Helping
Jamie is one of them, and I don't know how long he'll
need me. And you're right about my needing this job
here. I do. But I also want to go back to school soon.
Everything is in flux, so I was trying not to add something else to complicate my life."

"You think I'd complicate your life?" Hudson asked
with a crooked smile.

"I don't think it. I'm sure of it. But the more I get
to know you, the more I want the complication...the
more I want *you*."

His eyes darkened with that unsettling hunger
again. He seemed to take in a deep breath, as if he
was reminding himself not to hurry anything. "After
work, do you want to come back to my place?"

If she answered him affirmatively, she knew exactly
what she was agreeing to. Her hand on his arm, she
looked up at him with the wanting in her eyes.

She said simply, "Yes."

Hours later as Bella parked in back of Hudson's
vehicle and they walked together to the ranch house

door, he realized how surprised he'd been at her remark that this wasn't her first rodeo. He'd really thought she might be a virgin, not only because of her age, but because of her demeanor. But apparently he'd been wrong. Had she been hurt terribly by someone and that's why she held back?

After they entered the foyer, they were a bit awkward with each other. He wasn't going to just jump her bones, or rip her clothes off, or carry her to his bed, even though he wanted to do all three. More than anything, he wanted to do this right. Though he wasn't sure why that was so important.

He motioned to the great room. "Would you like something to drink?" he asked. "It might break the ice so we don't feel so rattled."

She smiled at that. "Something to drink would be nice."

"Hot chocolate, coffee, tea?" He wasn't going to suggest wine because he didn't want their senses dulled. He wanted to be aware of absolutely every moment tonight.

"Hot chocolate would be great." Looking nervous, she glanced around the room. Her eyes lit on the photo albums under the coffee table. "I saw these when I was here the last time. Do they belong to Mr. Bickler?"

"No, they don't. They're mine. Believe it or not, I take them wherever I go. Sometimes in a bunkhouse I might not have much else than my boots and my jeans and my sheepskin, and my Stetson. But keeping these with me when I travel helps me stay grounded. I remember I have a family, and I had a home where I grew up. It's just a way of remembering my roots."

"Do you mind if I page through them?"

He thought about that. "No, I don't mind. You'll have a good laugh at some of the pictures in there. They're candid shots, nothing like the photos you take."

"Candid shots are sometimes the best ones." She unzipped her parka, shrugged out of it and laid it over one of the chairs. Hudson felt himself relax. This evening was going to be everything he wanted it to be.

Hudson had learned hot chocolate was almost as important as hot coffee on a cold winter night. He'd become somewhat of a connoisseur and used a mix he special-ordered. Minutes later he carried in two mugs topped by a mound of whipped cream and sat on the sofa beside Bella, putting the mugs onto coasters.

She looked at the hot drink and smiled. "How did you know I liked whipped cream?"

"Just a good guess, I imagine."

She had a photograph album open on her lap. There were photos of him and his brothers as kids. His parents were in a few of them, but it was mostly just them.

"You and your brothers are *all* handsome," she murmured. She pointed to one of the pictures. "Who is who?"

He pointed to each in succession. "That's Autry, Gideon, Jensen and, of course, Walker."

Then she pointed to another picture. "Your mom and dad?"

"Yes."

Hudson's mother looked guarded in that particular photo. His father looked as imposing as ever with a shock of white hair and cold blue eyes. Yet Hudson knew he definitely bore a resemblance to them.

"You look like him—the same jaw, the same high forehead," she noted, mirroring his thoughts.

"I might look like him, but I hope we're different in lots of ways. He and Walker are more alike, all about business and money, maybe even power. Maybe that's why I took a left turn when they took a right."

"Do you respect them?"

"I respect Walker for what he's accomplished. And now he seems a bit different with Lindsay, as if he knows what matters. But my dad, maybe he's just been with the wrong woman all his life and they don't make each other happy. Or maybe they just don't want to work at it."

"I think about my parents often," Bella admitted. "If they had lived, I wonder if the Stocktons would be a close family. Would they have kept us all connected?" She looked up at Hudson. "The way it sounds, you and Walker might be different, but you *are* connected. That's why you're here helping him."

"That's why *you're* helping Jamie."

She nodded her agreement as she sipped the hot chocolate. He saw the whipped cream that gathered on her upper lip and suppressed the urge to lick it off. *Don't rush this. Let her get comfortable. You'll know when she wants you just as much as you want her.*

At least he hoped he would.

Bella placed her mug down as she swiped at her lips. "I have some good memories from before my parents died."

"Tell me," he encouraged her.

"There was this lake where Mom and Dad took us to go swimming. It had a grassy, stony shore, and the older kids would help the younger kids wade in. We had the best times there in the summers, swimming and picnicking. Jamie and I don't talk about those days much because it hurts to think about them. I guess because we miss our siblings. Yet I know remembering would be good for us, too."

Hudson pointed to a photo in the album. "I remember Walker and me being rivals at a lot of things. Roping a calf was one of them. Neither of us was very good at it at first, but our rivalry made us better."

Bella pointed to another photo of him inside a grand room. The Christmas tree he stood before had to be at least ten feet tall. "That's a beautiful tree."

"Mother always had a decorator come in and do the trees, along with other Christmas decorations. That's far different from a tree I'd like to bring in here for the holiday."

"What do you have in mind?"

"I want to go cut it myself and put it right over there." He pointed to a spot by the window. "When I told Greta I wanted to do that, she said she has a box of hand-crocheted white ornaments that she'd made one year for their tree. She has others that she uses now and she said I could have the crocheted ones if I'd like. I *would* like to use them, with lots of tiny lights."

"I'm sure the kids at Just Us Kids would make you ornaments if you asked them."

"I'm sure they would."

Suddenly it seemed that both of them had run out of conversation. Hudson couldn't take his eyes from Bella's, and it seemed Bella couldn't take hers from his. He slowly circled her with his arm and moved closer.

He could smell her floral perfume, like flowers in the middle of winter. Everything about Bella was sweet and pure. Sweeter and purer than he deserved.

"You can still change your mind," he whispered. And he meant it. He wanted nothing about tonight to be uncertain.

"I don't want to change my mind," she said with a small smile that made him ache even more with desire for her.

When he bent his head to her, when his lips captured hers, he felt possessive. He knew his mouth was claiming, and that's the way he wanted it. He wanted Bella to be his. He'd never been so in the moment with a woman before. He was excruciatingly aware of the softness of her skin as he stroked her cheek, the taste of chocolate on her tongue, the small moan that escaped her as they kissed. He gathered her into his arms and wondered how in the heck he was ever going to make it to the bedroom.

"I should have turned on the fireplace," he said when he broke for air.

"Or we could just keep warm under the covers," she suggested softly.

That did it. He rose to his feet and gathered her up into his arms. When he carried her to the bedroom, he felt like a caveman. Somehow Bella made him feel as if he could accomplish anything.

In his bedroom, he settled her on his bed. He found he didn't want to let her go even for a second. So he sat beside her, kissed her again and decided their clothes had to go.

"Light or dark?" he asked her before he started, curious as to what she'd say. The room was in shadows now, and they could hardly see each other's faces even with the hall light glowing.

"Let's turn on the light," she said. "I want to see your face."

Her response pleased him. Loving her in the light meant she felt free about what they were going to do. She felt right about being with him. There was no reason for darkness or shadows or hiding what they were feeling.

After he switched on the bedside lamp and fumbled with a condom packet from the drawer, he reached for her. Not long after, their clothes were on the floor and he'd turned back the covers and rolled on the condom. They were naked on the steel-gray sheets, and he soaked in the beauty of Bella's body.

"Are you cold?" he asked.

"No. Every time you touch me I feel like I'm on fire."

"Same here."

He palmed her breast, wanting her to be ready for him in every way. She moaned, and he kissed her again, this time covering her body with his. He ran his hand up her thigh and then teased her until she wrapped her legs around him.

"I can't wait," he said.

"I'm ready," she whispered.

And just like that, he was inside Bella and he felt as if he'd come home.

She held on to him tightly, but when he kissed her again, he was aware of tears on her cheeks.

"Bella?"

"It's wonderful. *You're* wonderful."

Her words drove him to prolong each stroke, to kiss her more passionately, to touch her everywhere he could. He held off his own pleasure until he felt her body tense, until he heard her cry his name, until she clung to him as if she'd never let him go.

Then he gave in and knew pleasure as he'd never known it before. With Bella in his arms, he felt as if he'd conquered the world.

Chapter Eleven

Bella awoke slowly, realizing where she was and whom she was with. Hudson's arms surrounded her as she lay on her side with him spooned against her. She held no illusions about what had happened last night. She had no expectations. Disappointed before, she didn't want to hope. Yet she couldn't help but remember each kiss, each touch, each word they'd exchanged.

She ran her hand lightly over the hair on his forearm, knowing in her soul that Hudson's strength was more than skin-deep. She admired the man. No, she more than admired him. She'd tumbled over a cliff and fallen in love with him.

Love. How long had it been since she'd known love from anyone other than her brother?

However, she suspected Hudson's feelings didn't run as deep. She'd learned the hard way that men's sexual desire often dictated their actions. Certainly Hudson was no exception. Wanting her and loving her were two entirely different things.

She thought Hudson was still asleep, but a light nip on her shoulder told her that he wasn't.

Could she face him and the fact that one night might have been enough for him? After last night, how would they react to each other at Just Us Kids? She'd followed her heart and now felt foolish.

She started to inch toward the edge of the king-size bed. Better to leave than to face the awkward conversation that told her it was over before it had begun.

But she didn't get very far. Hudson's arm tugged her back to him. He moved over a bit so she could turn to her back, and now she had no choice but to face him.

"Where do you think you're going?" he asked.

"I have to get dressed and go back to the ranch."

"It's not even sunrise," Hudson reminded her.

"When babies are hungry, they don't care if the sun's up or not. I told Jamie I'd be home this morning to help him."

Hudson studied her, then removed his arm from around her. "Do you want to go?"

Just what was Hudson asking her? To be vulnerable and lay her feelings out on the bed? She didn't know if she could do that. "I thought you'd want me to leave."

He stroked a wisp of hair behind her ear. "I don't want you to leave. If it was up to me, we'd stay here all day. I know we can't. We need to talk about how we're going to handle our relationship in public."

She felt heart-tugging joy that he wanted a relationship. Was it possible she could dream again and have that dream come true?

"We should probably keep this—" she motioned to

the bed and everything that had gone on there "—a secret."

"I thought you might say that, but I disagree. We have to think about our situation realistically. I would agree, no public displays of affection at work, even though at times I don't know how I'm going to resist kissing you."

She felt a blush start to creep into her cheeks.

He leaned forward, possessively captured her lips and said good-morning in a way that had her tingling all over.

When he broke the kiss and backed away, he asked, "See what I mean? You smile that certain way and I just want to pull you into my arms. I won't do that at work, but I don't want to be secret about us being together either. If someone sees you here, so be it. We're consenting adults. What we do on our off time is no one's business but ours."

"I don't know how much off time we'll have," she said honestly. "Yes, Jamie has help, and Fallon stayed late last night because he asked her to, but I can't do that often. I can't leave him in the lurch."

"Then I guess we'll just have to steal as much time as we can in between, including lunch hours. My truck is roomy, and the heat we generate should counteract the cold weather, don't you think?"

The idea of a quickie with Hudson was as exciting as spending all day here with him. His crooked grin told her he wasn't just daring her to have sex with him in the truck. He was serious about it.

"And just where would we park your truck?"

"Oh, believe me, I'd find us a secluded spot. And

the falls aren't so far out of town that we couldn't make
it there and back in an hour. If we put our minds to
being together, we *can* be."

He slid a hand under her and nudged her in his direction.

"You did say we were two consenting adults," she
drawled coyly. "And we could practice for that truck
rendezvous."

With a low growl, he grabbed a condom packet
from the nightstand. After she helped him roll it on,
he pulled her on top of him, then ran his hands down
her bare back. She could feel him against her, fully
aroused and ready whenever she was. Maybe that's
why he wanted her on top, so she could set the pace.
This morning her pace would be as fast as his. She slid
back and forth against him until he groaned.

"Keep that up and this will be the shortest rendezvous on record."

"Practice makes perfect," she teased and rubbed
against him again.

"Bella, really, if you don't stop—"

"I'm not going to stop," she warned him. "I'm as
ready as you are."

One look into her eyes and he was assured of that
fact.

She rose up on her knees and then guided him inside her. She watched pleasure overtake him. Her orgasm came quickly, surprising her.

"We're not done yet," he said as he continued to
stroke her. As she kept riding him, she found her body
tightening all over again, the tension mounting till she

thought she'd go wild. He pulled her down on him, and together they climaxed in a thunderous orgasm.

"Was that quick enough for you?" she asked after she'd collapsed on him.

"*Quick* enough but not *nearly* enough," he responded, and she smiled against his chest.

Hudson felt shaken up, off balance, unsettled and definitely out of his depth. Making love with Bella had blown his mind, and he couldn't seem to sort his thoughts or his feelings. He felt rattled to his core, though he thought he'd hidden it well. He'd tried to be practical about the whole thing. But now at work, catching glimpses of Bella now and then, he just wanted to pull her into his arms and take her to bed again.

Would they be able to work together? He wasn't sure. He had to think about their relationship at work, but he wasn't considering much more than that. The job in Big Timber? Bella's commitment to her brother? His own wanderlust? The questions seemed too big to fit into the mix right then.

Though it was the day before Thanksgiving and many of the kids were home with their families, it was almost noon by the time Bella left her desk. She came into his office, and he braced himself for the feelings that came rushing back when he saw her.

"Are you busy?" she asked.

"No more than usual. What can I do for you?" He hadn't meant the question to have a sexual undertone, but it seemed to.

She blushed a little. "We could talk about that later," she said and gave him a big smile.

He laughed, and that broke the tension—tension that had been caused by mind-blowing sex and possibly the consequences of it. But he didn't want to cut off whatever was happening between them, and apparently she didn't either.

"Jamie has help tonight, so I'm free...free for a few hours. I thought we could spend some time together."

When he didn't answer right away, she hurried to say, "It's okay if you don't want to. I just thought I'd ask." She turned to leave his office.

But he was out of his chair before she could reach the door and blocked her way. "You didn't even give me a chance to think about it."

"I didn't want to put you on the spot. It's okay if you have other things to do."

He was aware of where they were, in his office with glass windows, and teachers and kids not far away. So it wasn't as if he could hold her and reassure her.

"How would you like to put up a Christmas tree with me?" he asked.

"Really?"

He nodded. "Since we're closing early today, we'll have enough light to find one to cut down. Then I'll set it up. I have Greta's crocheted ornaments. We could buy a few more on the way to the Lazy B."

"Sounds good."

"If I didn't have glass windows where everybody can see in, I'd kiss you."

"Later," she said with a wink.

Again, he felt as if his world had rocked on its axis.

Later that afternoon, Hudson could see Bella was excited about the prospect of putting up a Christmas tree at his house. He wondered if she hadn't had many Christmas trees since her parents had died. Would her grandparents have even thought of getting a tree for two kids who needed a little Christmas?

After a stop for ornaments, they'd gone to the Lazy B, then to the stables. Now they were bundled up, riding on a buckboard to a stand of trees he'd seen while on his horse one day last week. "I'm glad we got to the general store early while they still had a collection of balls and garlands. I like your idea of blue and silver mixed with Greta's white ornaments."

"I've always wanted to decorate a Christmas tree with blue and silver," she said.

"Can you tell me why?"

"I remember one like that when my parents were still alive. Mom said it reminded her of heaven and the stars. I've always remembered that."

"Did you have Christmas trees after your parents died?" After all, if they were going to be in some kind of relationship, they should be able to ask the tougher questions.

She was quiet for a little while, but then she told him, "A Christmas tree was too much trouble for my grandparents. I snuck a little one into my room one year, after Grandma died, but Gramps said it would just make a mess and I should get rid of it."

"Did you?"

"No, I didn't," she said defensively. "I put it in my closet. Jamie and I couldn't get each other much. I used my spending money to buy yarn, and I knitted him a scarf. He gave me a card of barrettes for my hair, and we put our presents under the tree in the closet. That probably sounds silly to you."

He transferred the horses' reins to one hand and wrapped his arm around her. "It doesn't sound silly at all. The two of you were trying to make the day special."

After they rode a little bit farther, he asked, "Do you think Jamie will put up a tree this year?"

"I don't know. The triplets are still too young to understand what it would mean, even though they might like looking at all the lights. I'm afraid it would remind Jamie of his Christmases with Paula, so I don't even want to suggest it. If he decides to do it, then I'll certainly help him with it any way I can."

Hudson drew up in front of a stand of pines. He said, "We have to walk a little ways in."

"I wore my boots."

He laughed. He liked the way Bella seemed to take things in stride. He liked the way she was ready for a new adventure even if it was just cutting down a Christmas tree.

"Look around and see if you can find one you like. They might have bare spots from being too close to the other trees, but we can always fill that in with garland or ornaments."

While Hudson took a saw from the back of the buckboard, Bella forged ahead, circling the pines, one after another. He had to smile as she looked at each with a critical eye.

"Imagining those blue and silver balls on them?"

"You bet, and a silver star on the top. We were lucky they had one of those."

Yes, they had been. That silver star could make some of Bella's dreams come true. At least her Christmas tree dreams.

She called from around a pine, "If Jamie doesn't put up a tree, maybe I can bring the triplets over to see yours."

That thought startled him for a moment. The babies in his house. Well, not *his* house, technically. What kind of havoc could they wreak? But once he thought about it, he decided he wouldn't care. Having the babies and their laughter in his house would fill it in a way that it hadn't been filled before.

Bella called from the end of a row. "I think I found one. It will be perfect."

From Hudson's experience, rarely was anything perfect. But he had to admit, Bella had found a pretty nice tree. It was about eight feet tall with no gaping holes. Now all he had to do was cut it down.

As he told Bella to stand back and he scrambled under the tree with the saw, she asked, "Have you ever done this before?"

"Believe it or not, I once worked on a Christmas tree farm."

"Why am I not surprised?"

He looked up at her. She wasn't wearing a hat, and her hair was being mussed by the wind. Her eyes were bright. Her cheeks were pink from the cold air. She'd never looked more beautiful.

"I bet I have a few more surprises up my sleeve. Or maybe not exactly up my sleeve," he said with a wink.

"You're incorrigible."

"You're not the first to tell me that. I think that was my dad's favorite word for me."

"Did you purposely try to live up to that opinion?"

"Sure. It set me apart from the others."

While she was still shaking her head, he took the saw to the base of the pine. It took elbow grease and a bit of work, but a short time later, he called to Bella to step way back, and the tree fell.

"Do you need help carrying it?" she asked.

"No. You run ahead to the buckboard and get out of the snow or you're going to be an icicle."

"No more than you are," she shot back.

"All right, if you want to help, make sure the tarp's laid out across the buckboard. That way when we want to take it in the house, we can just wrap it in the tarp."

Bella made sure the tarp was spread from one side of the wagon to the other. It seemed to cause Hudson no stress at all to pick up the tree by its trunk and load it.

Once he had, she looked at it and said, "It's going to be a beautiful tree."

Beautiful. Just like her. As he looked at her, he felt a wet flake on his nose and realized snow was falling now.

"It's just like in the movies," she said with a laugh of sheer joy. "Cutting down the Christmas tree, putting it in the buckboard and having snow fall." She lifted her hands up to the heavens as if to catch a few flakes.

There were no glass windows around them now, and no one to see them for miles. He captured Bella in his arms and swung her around. "I've never cut down a tree quite like this before."

"What do you mean?"

"Oh, I've cut down trees, but not with someone I cared about. That changes everything."

Still, if he had to list what, he probably couldn't right then. He just knew that this seemed to be the start of something.

He was still holding her when he put her on the ground. "We could have a quickie out here," he whispered into her neck.

"And literally freeze our buns off?"

"Of all times for you to be practical," he grumbled.

"Of all times for us to think about whether we'd want the exciting experience of polar lovemaking, or if we'd rather go back to your place, switch on the fire and think about doing it there."

"Both are tempting," Hudson admitted with a joking air. "Snow, pines, the buckboard and a tarp. Or a glass of wine, a blazing fire, fewer clothes to fumble with."

"I think you're convincing me. But just to make sure, let's experiment a little."

With that he took her cheeks in his hands. They were as cold as his hands were warm. The sensation of touching her like this was a once-in-a-lifetime experience. They didn't kiss at first, but rather rubbed noses. They laughed and teased, snuck cheek kisses and neck kisses before they finally came together in a lip-lock kiss.

Bella had removed the top of her gloves. Although her palms were covered with fabric, her fingers weren't. She could dive her fingers into his hair that way. And when she did, he realized they were taking freedoms with each other, and that was good.

The snow began falling harder as they experimented, him burying his nose at the base of her throat and giving her a kiss there, her reaching her hands inside his coat so she was plenty warm. He could have stood with her all night like that, rocking back and forth, kissing, snuggling.

But the snow was becoming a fuzzy curtain of white now. He whispered close to her ear, "We have to get back."

She nodded as if she knew it were so, but she gave a sigh. What they had done had been fun. They'd just have to do it again sometime.

They both had snowflakes on their hair and their eyelashes by the time they returned to the house. Edmond was at the barn to help Hudson dismantle the buckboard and take care of the horse. Hudson suggested Bella go into the house instead of staying out in the cold. He'd bring the tree inside and set it up, and then they could start decorating.

Bella said, "I'll make hot chocolate to warm us up."

Hudson gave her a look that said they didn't need hot chocolate for that. Edmond no doubt caught the look because as soon as Bella left the barn, he gave Hudson a thumbs-up.

"Something's different between the two of you," he said. "Are you a couple now?"

Hudson shrugged. "We'll see."

Were they a couple now? That was a question to ponder while he set up the tree.

Less than an hour later, Bella watched Hudson string the lights on the tree. They'd chosen tiny white twinkle lights. She thought about their excursion to cut down the pine, and she had to smile. She was so glad Jamie hadn't needed her tonight. She was so glad she could do this with Hudson. She suddenly realized that she wouldn't want to be doing it with anyone else.

The problem was, she didn't know what Hudson expected next. For that matter, she didn't know what *she* expected next. Was this just an affair or a fling? Or could it be more? If it could be more, what would happen if she told Hudson she couldn't have children? Or that at least the likelihood of it happening was very slim?

He was great with kids, even babies, but as he turned to her now and said, "Ready for the ornaments," she pushed questions and doubts out of her mind. It had been years since she'd lived in the moment, and that's what she wanted to do now. Tomorrow, her world could crash down around her. For just today, she wanted to be happy.

Hudson took a break to sip his hot chocolate. "Yours is getting cold."

She went over to the coffee table and picked up her cup. She clinked her mug against his, then she turned toward the tree. "We're doing a fine job. Do we put the star on first or save it till last?"

"Let's save it till last. Are you getting hungry?" he asked. "I put that casserole Greta made into the oven."

"That sounds good," Bella agreed. "I'll start unpacking these ornaments." As she took blue ones from the box and attached little hooks to each one, she heard Hudson moving around in the kitchen. Then she heard the buzz of his cell phone and the rumble of his voice as he spoke with someone. But she couldn't hear the conversation.

Five minutes later he returned to the living room. His expression was thoughtful. "That was Walker on the phone. We were discussing Thanksgiving tomorrow. I know you'll probably want to spend it with Jamie and the triplets. Do you have plans?"

"It snuck up on us so quickly we didn't even buy a turkey. I told Jamie I'd stop at the store on the way home tonight to buy fixings for a dinner."

"I might have a solution for that. Walker and Lindsay want you and Jamie and the triplets to come to dinner at the Dalton ranch."

"All of us?"

"All of you. Lindsay has a huge clan who think the more the merrier. Do you think Jamie will go for it?"

"He might. It would be good for all of us to get out."

"Do you want to give him a call, then I can call Walker back?"

"Sure. I can check in and make sure everything's okay, too."

At first Jamie wasn't sure he wanted to join the Daltons, but then Bella said, "Don't you think it would be good to spend the holiday away and make a new memory?"

After a moment of silence, Jamie responded, "I suppose it would. All right. Tell Hudson to tell his brother he'll have five more at his table."

When Bella did, Hudson laughed. "Apparently it's going to be a big table." He approached Bella and motioned to the ornaments on the coffee table. "We'd better get to tree decorating. What time did you tell Jamie you'd be home?"

"I told him around nine."

Hudson stepped even closer. "When we have limited time together, we have to decide what's most important— decorating the tree, eating or..."

The *or* turned into a kiss that took Bella to a place where happiness was possible, where dreams could come true and where Hudson filled her world.

Hudson was passion and sensuality and all man. Hunger swelled inside her, a hunger like she'd never known. Conscious thought didn't seem possible as Hudson's tongue plundered her mouth, as she chased it back into his, as they kissed each other like they might never do it again. She slid her hands into his thick hair, then needing the touch of skin on skin, she massaged the nape of his neck. When Hudson slid his hand under her sweater, she wanted to give him freer access. She backed away slightly, and he broke the kiss.

"We have too many clothes on," he mumbled, finding the edge of her sweater and bringing it up over her head. After he tossed it onto the sofa, he just looked at her for a few moments.

She was glad she'd worn the bra edged with lace. He unhooked it, then he began unbuttoning his shirt. Not long after, they were on the floor in front of the fire, both naked.

"Decorating the tree seemed important when we were cutting it down, but now this is more important." He whispered his hot breath against her skin as he trailed his lips down to her nipple and suckled it.

Bella thought she was ready to make love with Hudson again. But he apparently had no intention of rushing it. He laid her back on the rug and swept her body with featherlight kisses and butterfly touches, sensual, heady and thrilling. Everywhere they touched, his hands ignited a heat that threatened to sear her skin. As his hands slid down her stomach to her thigh, exquisite sensations bombarded her. This much need, this much want and this much hunger couldn't be right, could it?

She didn't have an answer to that question because she'd never experienced anything like this before. She felt like one of the logs on the fireplace grate that glowed with an inner heat that couldn't be contained.

Although Bella could feel Hudson's hunger in his kisses and his touches, she could also feel tenderness. That's what undid her most of all. Leaning over her on the rug, Hudson kissed her once more while his hand slipped between her thighs. He wanted to see how ready she was. She passed her hand down his back to his backside and heard the growl that came from deep in his throat.

"Do you know what you do to me?" he asked her.

"Probably the same thing you do to me."

"Don't move," he said, sitting up, reaching for his jeans. She knew what he was doing. He was getting a condom from his pocket. She should tell him now. She should reveal that she could become pregnant yet would probably never be able to carry a baby to term. But she didn't say anything. She didn't want to spoil this day by ending it with a conversation that could separate them completely.

A minute later he was poised over her again, looking down into her shadowed eyes, and she wished she could take a picture of him right there and then. Then he entered her, and she held on to him tightly, wishing the moment could last forever. Wishing reality wouldn't poke its head back into her life. Wishing she'd been more responsible as a teenager so that she didn't have a secret to keep now.

She knew she couldn't keep the secret much longer because she wanted honesty between her and Hudson as much as she wanted anything else.

Chapter Twelve

Jamie's huge SUV maneuvered easily over a light coating of snow on the way to the Dalton ranch—the Circle D. It was located about a half hour out of town.

Bella glanced over her shoulder at the triplets, who were in their car seats behind her. "They seem content for the moment."

"Let's wait and see what happens when we get into a crowd. I'm not sure this was a good idea."

"They have to get out sometime, Jamie. Besides, did you really want to spend the holiday alone?" Sometimes she suspected it was more than protectiveness that kept Jamie from being out and about with his children. Was it grief or was there something else?

"I wouldn't have been alone," he said wryly.

"You know what I mean. Spending the day with the Daltons should be fun."

"We'll see," he responded, obviously not sure of that fact. He glanced at her quickly, then moved his eyes back to the road. "I think this was more about you spending the holiday with Hudson."

He had her there. Still, she said, "It's not like we'll have time alone."

"I'm sure you can steal a few minutes. You're getting more involved with him, aren't you?"

If "more involved" meant sleeping with him, yes, she was. But she wasn't willing to go into that with her brother.

When she was silent, Jamie said, "I worry about you."

"You don't have to."

"You gave up your life to help me. Of course I have to. You *are* going to go back to school, aren't you?"

"Eventually."

"Sooner, rather than later."

"Jamie, I don't know what's going to happen next."

"You mean with Hudson?"

She sighed. "With Hudson. With my job. With the triplets, even. I want to make sure you and the babies are stable before I consider doing anything else."

"We have our routine. We're doing well. If you go back to school, I'll look around for somebody else to help. Even if I have to pay them."

"You can't afford to do that. The ranch expenses are up, not to mention everything you need for the triplets."

"You're not trapped, Bella. I don't want you to think you are. I would figure something out."

She was sure he would. Still, she felt that he needed her.

"Did you tell Hudson yet about your miscarriage and your...problem?"

"No."

"How serious does it have to get before you do?"

"Everything with Hudson has happened so fast. I have to feel the time is right."

"The longer you wait, the harder it's going to be to tell him."

"I know," she said. But today wasn't going to be the day, not in the middle of a family Thanksgiving celebration. She was sure of that.

Shortly after their conversation ended, Jamie took the turnoff to the Circle D. At the fork in the road, Jamie said, "One of the Dalton brothers lives over there in that white house with the green shutters."

Each Dalton sibling was allotted land within the ranch borders. Although Ben Dalton and his wife, Mary, owned the ranch, Ben was a lawyer and didn't devote much time to it. His son Anderson was in charge and managed it for him. As Jamie drove a ways, Bella wondered what it would be like to belong to a large family and have everyone live close by. That would be nice.

After driving farther, Bella caught a glimpse of the stables. When they reached the main ranch house, she stayed in the car with Katie and Henry, while Jamie took Jared inside. She expected to see Jamie come back out, but instead Hudson did.

He approached the car door and said, "Your brother trusted me to help get the babies inside."

That was saying a lot, she supposed, because Jamie didn't trust just anyone with the triplets. They detached both car carriers from the backseat and carried them into the house.

Already there was a group of adults gathered around Jared, oohing and aahing. When Hudson and Bella brought the other two over, everyone made room. Lindsay and Walker welcomed them, and then the entire Dalton clan descended on them. The parents, Ben and Mary, as well as Anderson and his wife, Marina, with their blended family of eleven-year-old Jake and baby Sydney. There was brother Travis, a bachelor; Lani Dalton with her fiancé, Russ Campbell; and Caleb Dalton and his wife, Mallory, and their ten-year-old daughter, Lily. And, finally, Paige and her husband, Sutter, who cast watchful eyes over their two-year-old son, Carter.

In the center of the crowd, Lindsay smiled. "And this is just the tip of the Dalton iceberg. Uncle Charles is having Thanksgiving with his five kids. My other uncles, Phillip, Neal and Steven, have big families, too, but they live in another part of Montana."

Lindsay's mom, Mary, was particularly welcoming. She picked up Katie from her car carrier and said, "Aren't you pretty? With two brothers to treat you like a princess."

"Or pull her hair," her husband, Ben, said, and everyone laughed.

"We have high chairs so the triplets won't miss any of the celebration." She looked at Bella. "Do you want to come with me to see what else they might need?"

Hudson offered, "I can set up those high chairs."

"Thank you," Mary said. "Come on with me."

"I'll take Katie," Lindsay offered. She whispered to Bella, "It will do Walker good to be around babies."

For the second time in the last few weeks, Bella wondered if Lindsay might be wanting a child soon. Would Walker take to kids as his brother had?

Kids. It always came down to kids.

"What's wrong?" Hudson asked her as they followed Mary to the kitchen.

"Nothing," Bella said lightly. "I'm just hoping we can keep the triplets occupied during dinner so everyone can enjoy it."

"We can always take one out at a time and walk him or her. The Daltons are used to kids. I'm sure everyone will be sitting around the table long enough that a little excursion in and out with a baby won't spoil dinner at all."

In the kitchen, Mary pulled dishes from the cupboard, and Bella chose the ones she thought would be best for the triplets. "I have baby spoons in the diaper bag," she said. "Jamie will warm up their food right before we eat, if that's okay. He likes to maintain a stable diet for them."

"Maybe with a spoonful of mashed potatoes or two?" Mary asked with a twinkle in her eye.

"Maybe," Bella agreed.

A peal of laughter came from the living room, followed by lots of chatter.

"This is a real Thanksgiving," Hudson said.

"Your family doesn't get together for the holidays?" Mary asked him.

"My brothers are scattered all over now, and Mom and Dad are traveling. So, no, we don't. It's rare that even Walker and I are together."

"This *must* be a treat then. One of those holidays to remember. I'm glad you all could join us."

Hudson picked up one of the collapsed high chairs

that were leaning against a wall. "Any place special you want me to set this up?"

"No. Just fit them in wherever you can. I'm sure whoever is next to a baby will see to their needs. This is a child-friendly family."

Hudson carried a high chair into the dining room.

Mary turned to Bella. "What about you, child? I suppose you and your brother spend most of your holidays together."

"Yes, we do."

"I imagine this one is particularly hard for him. I hope being among friends will help. I've heard about the baby chain that takes care of the triplets."

"I don't know what we'd do without them. Not only in the care of the babies, but they've helped Jamie not draw into himself even more. They're kind and considerate, and he almost thinks of them as family now."

"One of the things I like most about this community is that we help others. I'm sorry that Lindsay and the day care center were at odds for a while. You know, don't you, that she was just doing her job?"

"Oh, I know that. I'm just glad everything turned out as well as it did."

"I hear that's your Hudson's doing."

"Oh, he's not *my* Hudson."

Mary laughed. "You can say that, but I see something else."

When Hudson returned to the kitchen for a second high chair, Bella knew her cheeks were flushed. When he left again, Mary said to her, "After dinner, when everyone's settling in to watch TV or chat, you and Hudson ought to take a walk down to the stables.

There's a new horse there you both might enjoy. Her name is Trixie…a fine quarter horse."

As Hudson returned to the kitchen, he heard the last part of that.

"Wouldn't you like to see our new horse?" she asked him.

"I'm always interested in a good horse. I'm sure Bella is, too. She doesn't just ride them, she photographs them. She did some work for the Smith Rescue Ranch."

"Really?" Mary asked.

"Jazzy and Brooks liked some of my shots, and they're using them on their pamphlets and on their website," Bella explained. "The redesigned website should be up by Monday. You should take a look if you get a chance."

"I'm not much into computers, but my husband and all my kids have them. So sure, I'll take a look. Now, come on. We have potatoes to mash, beans to dress and a turkey to carve."

When they were all finally seated around the table for the Thanksgiving meal, it was loud and fun. Many conversations traversed the room, and Bella couldn't keep track of them all. The triplets seemed mesmerized by all the people, let alone the food being passed around. So they were entertained while they ate.

She and Hudson had been seated next to each other. Every once in a while, Hudson would reach over and place his hand on her thigh. That simple contact sent a charge through her body, and she hoped it didn't show on her face. Now and then, however, she saw Lindsay looking at her speculatively. And one time Mary Dalton gave her a wink.

The talk among the men turned to ranching for a while. The women shared recipes, as well as caught up with their careers. Bella felt as if she were somewhere in between. Managing the day care center was not going to be her career. She took care of the triplets with Jamie and could easily discuss that. But she had her foot in two different worlds. Throw in her feelings for Hudson, and it was difficult to come up with a life plan, especially when she didn't know if he'd be staying or going...especially when she didn't know if he could accept not having children of his own.

She joined conversations, but her thoughts were jumbled. The only thing she did know was that she loved being with Hudson. She loved making love with him. She loved *him*.

By dessert time, the triplets were getting restless. Bella, Jamie and Paige took them from the high chairs and set them on their laps, distracting them with rattles and little toys.

Paige said, "The pageant on Sunday is going to be a hoot. Imagine all those babies, kids, costumes and Christmas."

"I'm going to have a look at the carriages tomorrow," Hudson said. "They're at the school and all decorated. I want to make sure there's nothing the babies shouldn't get hold of. I also need to get a few basic instructions to take to my staff. We aren't having a dress rehearsal with the rest of the group." He shrugged. "It's not as if our little ones have a script."

Everybody laughed.

"I'm sure they'll cause a lot of ad-lib moments," Ben said. "You can't have babies around and expect everything to go as planned."

"How about more whipped cream on that pumpkin pie?" Mary asked.

Mary and Ben had blocked off one area of the living room so the babies could crawl around and play with their toys in relative safety. Jamie sat on the floor with them, and Paige did, too. Jamie said to Bella, "If you want to go for a walk or anything, go ahead. We're fine for a while."

Paige waved at her. "We've got this."

Bella looked up at Hudson, who immediately got to his feet.

"I'll go get our coats," he said. "We'll take a look at that new horse."

As they made their way from the house to the barn, Hudson took Bella's arm. "Do you think you can get away for a few hours Saturday evening? I'd like to take you into Kalispell for a surprise."

"I'll have to talk to Jamie and see if he has other help."

"That's fine. I'd just like to take you on a real date. We can get dressed up, go to dinner, and then I'll show you my surprise."

Bella had no idea what Hudson was going to surprise her with, but whatever it was, the idea excited her.

The stables on the Circle D were a classic rectangular shape. Hudson opened the door for Bella and flipped on a switch just inside. The overhead light revealed a long center aisle with stalls on each side and a door at the other end, too. As they walked down the aisle, they saw plaques with the horses' names. They passed one for a giant black horse named Zorro.

"I think they have the heater on in here," Hudson said. "It's not as cold as outside."

Hudson was right, and Bella unzipped her parka as he unbuttoned his. They walked farther in, finally stopping in front of Trixie's stall. She was a cute little chestnut. The horse turned from her trough and gave them an interested look.

Bella held out her hand. "Come here, pretty girl. Let me pet you."

The horse apparently liked the sound of a friendly voice, because she turned and came to Bella, hanging her head over the slats so Bella could touch her nose. "No matter how many times I touch a horse's nose, I'm always amazed at the softness."

"I know what you mean," Hudson said. But there was a huskiness to his voice that made her think he was talking about her rather than the horse.

"You and Mary seemed to hit it off," he said.

"Yes, we did. She's nice."

He laid a hand on Bella's shoulder. "I feel for you that you lost your mother."

"Thank you. Lindsay's lucky. This whole family is lucky that they're still together and have each other."

"I think they realize that. Anderson does a great job managing the place. He wants to do it not just for himself, but for his family."

Bella had noticed more than the family atmosphere today. She'd noticed the couples in love—Lindsay and Walker, Anderson and Marina, Paige and Sutter, Caleb and Mallory. Had she been aware of them because of her own feelings for Hudson? If happily-ever-after was possible for *them*, maybe it was possible for *her*.

Suddenly she was very aware of Hudson beside her. He sidled closer and put his arm around her.

"Every time I'm close to you, I want to kiss you," he murmured in her ear.

She turned into his arms. "I feel like that, too."

Slowly he lowered his mouth to hers. This wasn't one of those quick let's-do-it-before-we-can't kisses. It was one of those I-want-to-take-my-time-with-you kisses. He began it softly but with the firm pressure of his lips. Seconds later, his tongue teased the seam of her mouth.

Her heart was beating so fast she couldn't breathe. But she didn't have to breathe. Not when Hudson was giving her his air, his taste, his desire. Her hand slipped into the collar of his jacket, felt his sweater and then the skin of his neck. Hudson's body was becoming more familiar now. She could feel the tension in it because of the need coursing through him, just like the need coursing through her.

His hand caressed the side of her face, then moved down her sweater to her breasts.

She nipped at his mouth, and he took that for assent of what he was doing. She was assenting all right. She couldn't seem to get enough of him. The stable seemed to spin around her, and she clung to Hudson as if he were the only thing in her world that was stable. He took her tongue deeper into his mouth, and she melted against him. His palm on her breast was replaced with his fingers as he kneaded her and searched for her nipple under the sweater. When he found it, she knew it was hard, and she could imagine him doing things to it with his tongue.

He groaned, dropped his hands to the waistband of the sweater and dived underneath. Skimming her stomach, they came to rest on her bra. Masterfully he flipped open the front catch, and then he was holding her, caressing her breasts, making her want him with a need so strong she could only hope it would soon be satisfied.

He said roughly, "I want you." He brought her hips tight against his so she could feel how hard he was and just how much he wanted her.

All of a sudden, Trixie neighed. The sound penetrated Bella's passionate haze. Then she heard bootfalls and the clearing of a throat.

"I was going to turn around and leave, but you might as well know that I know."

It was Walker's voice.

Hudson backed away slowly, but made sure Bella's coat was closed over her sweater. He wrapped his arm around her and faced his brother. "Don't you say a word," he warned Walker. "Not after what you and Lindsay did."

Bella knew her eyes were wide, and she felt stricken. No matter what Hudson had said, Walker owned the Just Us Kids franchise. Would her job be in jeopardy?

As if Hudson understood what she was thinking, he said to Walker, "This won't affect my working relationship with Bella."

Walker focused on Bella. "Your job is safe. You don't have to worry about that. No one could have handled everything as well as you have, especially with Hudson coming in to oversee you." He motioned to his brother and then to her. "In fact, this attraction between you might have helped that along, encouraged both of you to work for the good of the center."

"Then why does it matter that you *know*? You could have turned around and left and saved us a lot of embarrassment."

"I could have. But I still need to know if you're staying until Valentine's Day, or if you're going to leave before that for the job in Big Timber."

"And you have to ask me *now*?"

"Maybe it's a good thing I am, because Bella has to know, too, doesn't she? Or is she just another diversion until you're on your way?"

Bella's heart sank because Walker knew Hudson's history. And he knew Hudson's nature, too. If she was just a diversion, was she going to let their affair continue?

"I have to give Big Timber my answer on Monday," Hudson said. "I'll give you my answer then, too."

"So you haven't made up your mind?" Walker asked as if he expected nothing less.

"I'm still considering the pros and cons."

Again Walker looked from one of them to the other. And then he nodded and walked away.

They both heard the barn door close. They'd been so engrossed in their kiss, they hadn't heard it open.

Quickly Bella reached under her sweater and fastened her bra. She moved away from Hudson, thinking about everything Walker had said. Then she looked up at the tall cowboy and asked, "So you really don't know yet if you're staying or going?" Though she knew that if he stayed until Valentine's Day, that didn't mean he was going to stay longer.

He took her by the shoulders. "Bella, there's a lot to think about. Believe me, I'll tell you before I tell anyone else what I decide."

She supposed that was something, but it certainly wasn't enough.

"Are we still on for our date Saturday night?" he asked.

She thought of saying no and ending it then, so she could start nursing her heart back to health. But her heart wouldn't let her say it.

"Yes, we're still on for our date." Whether he stayed or whether he left, she loved Hudson Jones. For this weekend, that was going to be all that mattered.

Hudson glanced over at Bella on Saturday evening as she stared out the front windshield, eagerly anticipating where they were going. So far, everything had gone smashingly well. She'd joined him at the dress rehearsal for the pageant, so she'd be able to give teachers direction, too. Although there was tension between them because his decision about Big Timber was still in the offing, they'd seemed to put that aside during the dress rehearsal as well as at dinner tonight.

He'd taken her to the fanciest restaurant in Kalispell. She'd dressed festively in a beautiful long-sleeved red dress. Although the dress seemed modestly cut, its folds accented all her curves in just the right places. When he'd picked her up, she'd looked at him as if he were some kind of *GQ* model, which was crazy since he was wearing a Western-cut suit and bolo tie, a Stetson and boots. She'd given him a smile that had practically twirled his bolo.

Dinner was incredible, but the night wasn't over. He still had one more destination. To make conversation while he drove, he asked, "Do you think we're really ready for the pageant tomorrow? All those babies and kids at one place at one time—"

"We're as ready as we're ever going to be. Sometimes the more you regiment children, the more chaos you provoke. For the most part, all we have to do is make sure the babies are in their carriages and hope that the carriage decorations don't fall off. The one that looked like Santa's sleigh was pretty elaborate."

"The older kids really worked hard on them." Hudson was finding that he liked kids more and more... from babies to high-schoolers. And when he thought of kids, he thought of Bella. He didn't examine that thought too closely because he knew exactly where it might lead—Bella as a mom, him as a dad, a family like the Daltons had someday.

He glanced at Bella again and decided to concentrate on the here and now—on his attraction to her and on her surprise.

There were several cars parked in front of the building already. He pulled up to the curb in front of a bakery storefront.

Bella looked puzzled as he went around his truck and helped her out. She was wearing high-heeled boots, and he didn't want her to slip or fall.

"The bakery's closed," she said in a puzzled voice.

"We're not going to the bakery. I'd have you shut your eyes, but there are some icy spots."

"Why would you want me to shut my eyes?"

"You aren't used to surprises, are you?"

"Not good ones."

Hooking his arm into hers, he guided her along the sidewalk until they came to the Artfully Yours gallery. She looked up, saw the name and blinked. "You want to buy a painting?"

"You never know," he said with a smile.

They went up the steps, and he opened the door to lead her inside. At first, there didn't seem to be a huge selection. The gallery owner was selective on what he hung where, on what sculptures he positioned on pedestals.

The gallery manager came to greet Hudson, and they shook hands. Hudson had spoken with Jim Barringer on the phone several times. Jim gave Hudson a nod, and he led Bella to a side exhibit set in an alcove.

"Aren't you going to let me look at the paintings?" she started to ask, but then her eyes settled on the photographs hanging in the alcove. "Oh my gosh! They're mine. My photos. They're matted and framed."

"As well they should be. This isn't your own show... yet. But it is a showing. Notice the little red dots on two of them? That means they're sold."

Bella's mouth dropped open as she noticed the two sold prints—the landscape she'd shot at sunrise at the Stockton ranch and the close-up of one of the horses. The frames were perfect, rough-hewn like barn wood.

Bella turned to Hudson. "Did you do this?"

Hudson wondered again if he'd been too high-handed by doing it without her permission.

But then she threw her arms around his neck. "I can't believe you did this."

He squeezed her hard. "I didn't do the framing. I left most of that up to Jim, though he did ask my opinion. I just happened to know the gallery owner and asked him to take a look at your photographs. He thought they were well worth showing. You could have more than one career, if you want it, Bella."

Unmindful of where they were and who was around, Bella gave him a smacking kiss on the lips. When she broke away, she said, "Thank you."

"I'd do it again for another kiss like that," he teased.

She looked around the gallery. "I can't believe my photographs are hung here with all these talented artists."

"You're talented, too. You have to know that."

"Maybe I'm starting to."

For the next hour, they went from painting to painting…from sculpture to sculpture…from photograph to photograph until Bella had her fill.

On the drive back to Rust Creek Falls, Hudson thought that Bella might want to call Jamie and tell him her news. But she didn't. She just kept glancing at him, putting her hand on his thigh, looking at him as if he was Christmas all wrapped up in a cowboy package.

"Do you want to stop at my place?" he asked as they neared town.

"More than anything," she answered with such fervor that it took Hudson's self-control to the limit not to press down hard on the accelerator.

When they reached his house, he hurried out of the truck, going around to her side. When he opened her door, he saw longing in her eyes, too. He lifted her down from the truck and held on to her as they walked to the door. He fumbled with the keys as he tried to get the door open. All he could think about was holding her in his arms...naked. Time alone with her was precious, and honestly, he didn't know how much more they'd have.

After he punched in the code for the alarm, he took her into his arms, kissing her the way he'd wanted to kiss her all night. The ride home had seemed endless. He shrugged off his jacket, letting it fall to the floor. She was still unzipping her parka when he helped push it from her shoulders and let that fall, too. Her breath and his heightened and so did every look between them, every brush of their fingers, every touch of their skin. Bella's ability to return his hunger still amazed him. She undid his tie while he found the zipper at the back of her dress and ran it down its track. She unbuttoned his shirt while he pushed her dress down off her shoulders. It weighed on her arms as she was trying to undress him.

He laughed and said, "I can probably do it faster."

By the time he finished undressing himself and her, their clothes lay in a pile in the foyer. They couldn't seem to wait to reach the living room to touch each other. When her hands slid up his chest, he was a goner. He kissed her hard, and she returned his fervor, clutching his shoulders, pressing against him until he thought he'd die from the wanting. Lacing his fingers into her hair, he angled her head for another kiss.

When he broke away this time, she murmured, "I'm ready. We don't have to wait."

"Yes, we do," he said. "I have to grab a condom. Don't move."

She didn't.

"Turn around," he said, and she followed his gentle order, bracing her hands on the wall.

He wanted to give Bella every experience, every pleasure, every peaked orgasm. He just had to hold on a little longer. Stepping close behind her, he ran his hands over her breasts, teased her nipples, then slid his hands down her sides to her hips.

She understood what he wanted to do, and in the next second, he was thrusting inside her, pulling back, then doing it again until she moaned with as much pleasure as he felt. The wall braced them both as he felt her release come first, and then his followed. He rested his chin on her shoulder, and then he just held her.

When he could breathe again almost normally, he said, "Now we can try that in bed and take it a little slower."

She turned into his arms, wrapped hers around his neck and placed a kiss on his lips so tender that he thought he'd fall apart at the seams.

Scooping her up into his arms, he carried her to the bedroom, wanting to make each moment they had together last as long as it could.

Chapter Thirteen

On Sunday afternoon, Hudson felt a bit like a horse in the midst of a cattle stampede. It looked and felt as if everyone in Rust Creek Falls had come to the holiday pageant! That was understandable, he guessed, since the pageant was an important event and there wasn't much else in the way of entertainment in the small town.

Chairs had been set up in rows in the elementary school gymnasium with an aisle down the center. Teachers and volunteers milled about backstage along with a few parents, under the watchful eye of Eileen Bennet.

Classes from the elementary school had already performed. Scenery for the production had been swiveled around for two different segments. The first was an old-time scene where kids in costumes from the 1900s paraded onto the stage. The audience had been invited to sing traditional Christmas carols. The second segment depicted the 1960s with women and girls dressed in maxi-coats, fur rimming their hoods, and men in peacoats. More carols accompanied by the piano had brought a rousing response from the audience.

Now the audience awaited the third and last segment, a modern-day rendition of the holidays. In this segment, children would parade across the stage in Christmas finery. Bella had decked herself out in her red dress. Hudson had complied with the theme by wearing a green sweater and black jeans. Other teachers had dressed in holiday colors, and they would push the decorated carriages onto the stage. They would be followed by a wagon with kids and, of course, Santa Claus, who was actually one of the big, burly, white-bearded dads.

From the sidelines, Hudson heard one of the teachers call, "Quentin spit up! Paper towels, quick."

Another teacher shouted, "Mary's carriage is supposed to be in line before Monica's. Switch them. The parents know the order and will be upset if we don't have it right."

Bella, who was two carriages behind Hudson's, caught his eye. She gave him a thumbs-up and smiled. That smile. He remembered the sleepy expression on her face and the sparkle in her eyes after they'd made love last night.

Suddenly the baby in Bella's carriage lifted up his arms to her. She didn't hesitate to lift him out even though they were almost ready to go on. A baby's needs would certainly take priority over the pageant. She cuddled him and cooed to him, straightened his reindeer antlers and set him back in the carriage, handing him a rattle.

Hudson suddenly felt the need to go to her. Snagging the attention of Sarah Palmer, he asked, "Can you watch this young gentleman for a moment? I need to talk to Bella."

"Sure," Sarah agreed. "We have about five minutes until we push our carriages out onto the stage."

Going to Bella's side, Hudson asked, "How do you think things are going?"

"Great, so far. The audience is really involved. Now, if not too many babies cry once the carriages are on the stage, we'll have succeeded."

He chuckled, then looked over the scene before him with all the carriages lined up and children and teachers milling about. He motioned to the carriages. "I remember all the rumors about how these babies were conceived because of the wedding punch at Jennifer McCallum and Ben Traub's wedding. Supposedly, Homer Gilmore spiked it with a magic potion and there were lots of romantic hookups because of it. When I first came to town, I heard that some couples came here who were hoping to have a baby because they thought the magic might rub off on them."

Bella's face suddenly took on an odd expression. The sadness was back in her eyes, and he didn't understand any of it. But he did understand one very important thing, as if a lightning bolt had hit him. He never wanted her to be sad. He wanted to protect her...forever. He realized that he loved Bella Stockton, and he was going to do something about it.

Someone near the curtain gave a signal, and he gave Bella's arm a squeeze. "I have to get back to my carriage. See you after?"

She nodded and said, "Sure."

A few of the babies did cry as the carriages rolled out in front of Santa and the children on the stage sang "Jingle Bells" with the audience. Hudson, however, wasn't living in the moment right now. All he could do was stare at Bella and wish the pageant was over. He had something to say to her, and he couldn't wait to say it.

He should have seen his love for her before now, but maybe he'd been blinded by the chemistry between them, by the passion that seemed to supersede everything else when he was around her. Bella Stockton was everything he'd ever wanted in a woman without even realizing it. She was smart and challenging and sweet. Most of all, she knew how to care and she knew how to love. That was evident in her loyalty to her brother, her love for the triplets, her care of every child at Just Us Kids.

Hudson realized now that home wasn't so much a place. It could be a person. He wanted to make Bella his home and hoped she felt the same about him. He realized now he could make a life in Rust Creek Falls with her, and he had an idea about that. He was going to get on his cell phone and make sure that dream could come true as soon as he talked to Bella. Maybe he'd always been a rich man, but he hadn't felt rich before. With Bella by his side, he knew he could be a better man than he'd ever been. They'd raise a family together, and they'd hand down values that could last through the years. She'd never said how many kids she might want, but he didn't care about that. Two, four or five. They'd talk about it. They'd kiss about it. They'd make love about it.

Hudson spotted Walker and Lindsay in the audience. Not far away, he spied Jamie with the triplets in their stroller. Fallon was with him. Hudson gave him a big smile and a thumbs-up, and Jamie grinned back. The green headband on Katie's little blond hair tilted sideways. Jamie straightened it with such a loving expression on his face that Hudson knew he couldn't wait to be a dad. Would Bella want to have kids right away, or wait awhile? There was so much to talk about, so much to look forward to, so many dreams to fulfill.

With all the people and babies and kids involved in the pageant, it was almost an hour later until the scenery had been stowed in the wings, until parents had been reunited with their children, until the audience who had come to mingle as well as to watch the show drifted out of the auditorium.

Bella, who had helped stow the babies' reindeer headbands in a plastic bin, snapped on the lid and stacked it with boxes that held other costumes. Hudson was about to burst with what he wanted to say to Bella.

As they walked to the exit, he cloaked his excitement and asked her, "Do you have to get back to the ranch right away?"

She zipped up her parka and hoisted her hobo bag over her shoulder. "I do," she said. "Fallon helped Jamie at the pageant, but she can't stay. I told Jamie I'd be there to help feed and bathe the babies."

Hudson felt a pang of disappointment, but he knew this was Bella's life. They'd have to talk about that along with everything else. But right now, he had to take a few minutes to tell her how he felt. He couldn't hold it in any longer.

"I know we don't have much time..." He took her hands in his. "But I want you to know how much last night meant to me."

"It meant a lot to me, too," she responded. "I can't thank you enough for recommending me to Artfully Yours. But beyond that, Hudson, I've never spent time with a man like you."

"And I've never spent time with a woman like you. And because of that, I have to tell you something, Bella." He drew in a shaky breath and then went for it. "I love you. I want to marry you and make a life with you that includes lots of babies." He gave her a broad smile. "Will you marry me?"

Hudson expected an enthusiastic "yes." He expected Bella to throw her arms around his neck and say that she loved him, too. He expected they'd both be hearing wedding bells instead of silver bells. But none of those things happened. Instead, Bella burst into tears, turned away from him and pushed out the exit door.

It took him a moment to realize what had happened. The door had swung shut, and he pushed out after her.

"Bella, wait," he yelled.

But she was headed to her car.

He took off at a run after her, but when he caught up to her at the driver's side door, she was shaking her head. "I can't give you want you want. Not ever."

Hudson was so shell-shocked he couldn't move, think or talk. In the next few moments, she started the engine, backed up and drove away.

Just what had caused *that* reaction? More important, what was he going to do about it?

* * *

Hudson spent the rest of the evening trying to decide the best thing to do. He could make Bella face him, but he wasn't sure that would do any good. She had to *want* to talk to him. He didn't want to force her.

That evening when his cell phone beeped, he grabbed it up, hoping beyond hope it was Bella. But Jamie Stockton's number showed up.

"Jamie, is Bella all right?" he asked before the rancher could get a word out.

"She asked me to call you. She's taking a sick day tomorrow."

"A sick day? To avoid me?"

He heard Jamie's sigh. Hudson knew Bella might be right there and her brother couldn't talk freely. With insight, he realized talking to her brother might be better than talking to Bella right now.

He asked, "Can you get an hour away at lunch tomorrow?"

Jamie responded cautiously, "I might be able to. Why?"

"Can you meet me at the Ace in the Hole? I need to talk to you about Bella. I only want the best for her. I love her, Jamie."

"All right," Jamie said.

"Around one okay?" Hudson asked.

"If it's not, I'll let you know."

Jamie ended the call without saying more, and Hudson knew Bella was probably listening and Jamie didn't want her to know about their meeting. She might feel her brother was betraying her.

Hudson didn't want to cause a rift between them, but he had to find out what was going on.

The next morning dragged on so slowly Hudson could count each second. He left for the Ace in the Hole fifteen minutes early, found a table there, ordered coffee and drummed his fingers until Jamie Stockton walked in the door.

Jamie saw him and headed toward the table. After he unzipped his jacket, he looked at Hudson's coffee. "I thought you might be drinking something stronger."

"I need a clear head for this conversation," Hudson said. "I need a clear head for this whole situation."

Jamie signaled a waitress and pointed to Hudson's coffee and at his own place. She nodded. Seconds later, he had a mug of black coffee in front of him, too.

"What's on your mind?" he asked Hudson.

"We need to talk, man-to-man, brother to the man who loves your sister."

"I don't know if a talk will do any good," Jamie said.

Hudson felt there was a closed door in front of him, but he wasn't going to let it stay closed. He was going to open it. Heck, he was going to push through it. "Look. I know Bella has a lot of baggage. I want to know the best way to help her deal with it."

Jamie eyed him and asked, "What do you want?"

"I want a future with her. I want a life with her—a family and kids."

A shadow passed over Jamie's face, the same shadow that Hudson had seen on Bella's. Then Jamie seemed to make up his mind. "Yes, Bella has a lot of baggage. She felt abandoned like I did when our parents died. She felt rejected when our grandparents didn't want our siblings and didn't want us either, though they took us in. But her hurts aren't as simple as all that."

"Simple? There's nothing simple about being abandoned. What else is there?"

"I'm only telling you this because I think it's best for Bella. She rebelled against our grandparents' rejection. She became a little…wild. She looked for love in the wrong places. She got pregnant, and she had a miscarriage. Because of that miscarriage, she probably will never be able to have children."

If Hudson had been shocked by Bella's response yesterday, he was even more shocked by what Jamie had told him. He felt numb. She might never be able to have children? It was so much to take in, and he didn't know how he felt about all of it.

He thought about how intimate he and Bella had been, and he couldn't help but mutter, "Why didn't she trust me enough to tell me?"

"I think you can answer that yourself. For a lot of years, I don't think she's trusted anybody but me."

"I feel so sorry for her."

"But?" Jamie asked with a probing look.

"My heart hurts at the idea of not having kids with her."

"That's why I told you this. If you can't deal with the idea of no kids, then you should walk away now. Don't hurt Bella further by rejection later." He nodded to Hudson's coffee cup. "Do you want something stronger than that now?"

Hudson glanced at the bar and all the bottles behind

it. "No, I still need a clear head to think this through. Thanks for your honesty."

Jamie picked up his mug, took a couple of swallows of coffee and set it back down. As Bella's brother rose to his feet and then left, Hudson was hardly aware of it. He was too lost in his thoughts.

The sun was barely up the next morning when Bella stood at Hudson's door and rang the bell. She was shaking. She didn't know if this was the right thing or the wrong thing to do. She didn't know if Hudson would even let her inside after the way she'd left him.

When he didn't answer the door, Bella wondered if he'd gone riding or already left for the day. She could check the garage to see if his truck was there.

Just as she was about to do that, the door opened and Hudson stood there, his expression totally unreadable. She could tell one thing, though. He looked tired, as if she'd gotten him out of bed. His hair was sleep-mussed, there was a heavy stubble on his jaw and his feet were bare under a pair of sweatpants.

"I'm sorry if I woke you," she said.

"No harm," he returned evenly.

She wasn't sure about that. "May I come in?"

He ran his hand through his mussed hair and pulled down his T-shirt. "I haven't even had a cup of coffee yet. Are you sure you want to talk to me now?"

There was an edge of something in his voice, and she supposed she deserved that. She hadn't wanted to talk to him Sunday or yesterday. Coffee or not, she'd take her chances today.

"Yes, I need to talk to you."

His eyebrows arched at the words. He backed up in the foyer so she could enter.

After she did, she closed the door behind her, wishing he'd react more, say something, do something. Like kiss her?

That was wishful thinking.

She had done nothing but think and cry and worry since she'd left him Sunday. She'd helped Jamie with the triplets but told him she didn't want to talk about any of it. She couldn't, not until she figured out what she was going to do. Jamie had pretty much left her alone because he'd known this was her problem to solve and her life to lead. All she could think about all day yesterday and last night was how her heart hurt because she loved Hudson so much. She loved him enough to walk away if that's what he wanted. But she had to be honest with him, and she had to tell him everything first. That was only fair after what they'd shared.

Hudson led her into the living room and sat in the armchair. Maybe he expected her to sit on the sofa, but she didn't want to be that far away. She needed to make eye contact with him, and she needed to be close. So she sat on the large ottoman in front of him.

He looked surprised and maybe a bit uncomfortable.

How could she mess this up any more than she already had? But she wasn't going to scurry away now. "I'd like to tell you...everything."

"Everything?"

"You know most of it, but..." She couldn't lose her courage now. She plunged right into her story. "I felt so lost after my parents died."

She thought she saw a glimmer of compassion in his eyes, but she couldn't be sure. But she hadn't come here for pity, so she hurried on. "Jamie and I missed our five other brothers and sisters. It was like one minute we had a family and the next we didn't. Grandma and Gramps didn't want us, and..." She lifted her hands as if she didn't have to explain any more about that. "I told you I was wild, and you didn't believe me, but I was. I'm not the woman you thought I was, Hudson. When I was a teenager, I wasn't smart or mature. I was fifteen, and I ended up dating and sleeping with an older boy."

"How old?" Hudson asked, and she couldn't tell if there was judgment there or not.

"He was almost eighteen. I got pregnant. I thought he loved me. I thought we'd have a family. But I was so stupid. He didn't want any responsibilities. When I told him I was pregnant, he said it wasn't his."

"You could have proved otherwise."

"I could have. My guess is Gramps would have made me prove it to get child support. But we never had to do that." She heard the quaver in her voice and swallowed hard. When she spoke again, she'd regained her composure. The only way she'd get through this was to blurt it out. "There were complications with the pregnancy. I lost the baby, and the doctor said I might never be able to have another one. I have a weak cervix. I can possibly *get* pregnant, but I'd never carry the baby to term."

Before Hudson could say anything, she pushed on. "My grandparents kept the whole thing secret. I wasn't showing when the miscarriage happened, and I certainly hadn't told anybody but the boy, and he wasn't saying anything to anybody. After Grandma died, Gramps said I caused her heart attack with the stress of my pregnancy and what happened afterward. That's what killed her."

"He was wrong," Hudson said with more expression than she'd heard yet.

"I don't know if he was or not. The only saving grace was that my parents weren't alive to see it."

"If your parents had been alive, the whole situation probably wouldn't have happened," Hudson reminded her.

"I know you probably think less of me now. I know you probably want your own children more than you want me. It wasn't fair that I didn't tell you about all this before we made love."

Suddenly Hudson moved forward in his chair and took her hands into his. "I already know about all of this."

She felt as if the breath had been knocked out of her. Recovering, she asked, "How could you?"

"I had a talk with Jamie yesterday. I don't think he wanted to tell me. He wanted you to confide in me. But he also didn't want you hurt any more than you already were."

"Maybe I should go," she said softly and tried to pull away from him.

But he held on to her and wouldn't let her move. She was as mesmerized by the look in his eyes as she was by the hold of his hands.

"I thought a lot about us in the past two days, Bella, and I know exactly what I want."

She held her breath as panic seesawed in her stomach.

"I love you. I don't want to live without you. I would be fine with adopting kids if that's what you want to do. If you want biological children, there are ways to make that happen. There are advantages to being rich, you know. I can have access to the best doctors in the world, or we can hire a surrogate."

Tears burned her eyes, and she felt a few roll down her cheek.

He went on. "Did I mention that I love you and I can't live without you?"

She was full out crying by then and so in shock she couldn't move or speak until he asked, "Will you marry me, Bella Stockton? Make a family with me? Grow old with me?"

Now the look in his eyes sunk in. It was the look of love. It warmed her, surrounded her and made her free.

"Yes," she said jubilantly. "Yes, I'll marry you!"

Hudson gathered her into his arms and held her on his lap. Then he kissed her with so much promise that she knew she'd remember this day forever.

Epilogue

Hudson and Bella, filled with the Christmas spirit, were decorating Just Us Kids for the holiday. They'd erected an artificial tree in the lobby and were adding ornaments, one by one, their fingers brushing often, their gazes connecting.

They were still working out their plans to get married. Hudson was hoping Jamie would accept some financial help to hire someone to take Bella's place with the triplets. He'd talked to Jamie about it, and Jamie said he'd consider it. Bella's brother was just happy that she was finding happiness.

Hudson had a couple of surprises for her and decided now was as good a time as any to produce one as they put the finishing touches on the tree. Bella had wrapped empty boxes to place underneath it in bright shiny paper and pretty ribbon. It had been only three days since she'd accepted his marriage proposal—three days of giddy happiness, work and, last night, a long night of lovemaking.

Taking a box from his pocket that was wrapped in silver with a gold bow, he handed it to her. "The bow's a little smashed," he said, "But I didn't want you to see it before now. Open it."

"It's early for a Christmas present," she teased.

"We're going to have one long Christmas," he assured her.

She took the bow from the box and set it aside. Then she unwrapped the silver paper and did the same with that. Taking the lid from the black box, she found a velvet-covered one inside.

She looked up at him.

He saw her fingers tremble as she opened the ring box. Inside, on white velvet lay a platinum ring with a large center diamond and tiny diamonds circling it. It reminded Hudson of a snowflake.

He explained, "I hope you like it. I saw this ring at the jewelers, and it reminded me of that day we went riding and the snow started falling. I wanted something unique for you. What do you think?" He took it from the box and slipped it onto her finger.

Bella's face was glowing as she said, "I think it's perfect."

"I hope you'll think something else is perfect," he suggested.

"Uh-oh, another surprise."

"I hope it's a good one. I'm buying Clive Bickler's ranch. We'll have a real home and a place to ride and lots of room to raise a family."

Bella had hung a ball of mistletoe in the doorway of Hudson's office. Taking his hand, she led him to it now. On tiptoe, she wrapped her arms around his neck and gave him a kiss Hudson knew he'd long remember.

His fervor was exploding into downright fiery passion when he heard a noise. Still holding Bella, he broke the kiss slowly, then turned toward the lobby. There were two moms there with strollers with babies. They were grinning from ear to ear.

But Hudson didn't care. He was ready to shout from the mountaintops that he loved Bella Stockton and she was going to be his wife. Bella must have felt the same way because she drew his head down to hers again and kissed him once more.

They were going to have the merriest Christmas of both of their lifetimes.

* * * * *

Don't miss the next installment of the new Special Edition continuity

MONTANA MAVERICKS: THE BABY BONANZA

Everyone has rallied behind Jamie Stockton as he raises his triplets alone—including his lifelong friend Fallon O'Reilly. She's loved him from afar since they were kids. Will Christmas bring the babies a new mommy?

Look for
THE MORE MAVERICKS, THE MERRIER!
by
award-winning author Brenda Harlen

On sale December 2016,
wherever Harlequin books and ebooks are sold.

COMING NEXT MONTH FROM

♦ HARLEQUIN®

SPECIAL EDITION

Available November 22, 2016

#2515 THE HOLIDAY GIFT
The Cowboys of Cold Creek • by RaeAnne Thayne
Neighboring rancher Chase Brannon has been a rock for Faith Dustin since her husband died, leaving her with two young children. Now Chase wants more. But Faith must risk losing the friendship she treasures and her hard-fought stability—and her heart—by opening herself to love.

#2516 A BRAVO FOR CHRISTMAS
The Bravos of Justice Creek • by Christine Rimmer
Ava Malloy is a widow and single mother who is not going to risk another heartbreak, but a holiday fling with "hunky CEO Darius Bravo sounds just lovely! Darius wants to give her a Bravo under her tree—every Christmas. Can he convince Ava to take a chance on a real relationship or are they doomed to be a temporary tradition?

#2517 THE MORE MAVERICKS, THE MERRIER!
Montana Mavericks: The Baby Bonanza • by Brenda Harlen
Widowed rancher Jamie Stockton would be happy to skip Christmas this year, but Fallon O'Reilly is determined to make the holidays special for his adorable triplets—and for the sexy single dad, too!

#2518 A COWBOY'S WISH UPON A STAR
Texas Rescue • by Caro Carson
A Hollywood star is the last thing Travis Palmer expects to find on his ranch, so when Sophia Jackson shows up for "peace and quiet," he knows she must be hiding from something—or maybe just herself. There's definitely room on the ranch for Sophia, but Travis must convince her to make room in her heart for him.

#2519 THE COWBOY'S CHRISTMAS LULLABY
Men of the West • by Stella Bagwell
Widowed cowboy Denver Yates has long ago sworn off the idea of having a wife or children. He doesn't want to chance that sort of loss a second time. However, when he meets Marcella Grayson, he can't help but be attracted to the redheaded nurse and charmed by her two sons. When Marcella ends up pregnant, will Denver see a trap or a precious Christmas gift?

#2520 CHRISTMAS ON CRIMSON MOUNTAIN
Crimson, Colorado • by Michelle Major
When April Sanders becomes guardian of two young girls, she has no choice but to bring them up Crimson Mountain while she manages her friends' resort cabins. Waiting for her at the top is Connor Pierce, a famous author escaping his own tragedy and trying to finish his book. Neither planned on loving again, but will these two broken souls mend their hearts to claim the love they both secretly crave?

YOU CAN FIND MORE INFORMATION ON UPCOMING HARLEQUIN® TITLES, FREE EXCERPTS AND MORE AT WWW.HARLEQUIN.COM.

HSECNM1116

*Chase Brannon missed his first shot at a future with
Faith Dustin, but will the magic of the holiday season
give him a second chance?*

*Read on for a sneak preview of
THE HOLIDAY GIFT,
the next book in* New York Times *bestselling author
RaeAnne Thayne's beloved miniseries,
THE COWBOYS OF COLD CREEK.*

"You're the one who insisted this was a date-date. You
made a big deal that it wasn't just two friends carpooling
to the stock growers' party together, remember?"

"That doesn't mean I'm ready to start dating again, at
least not in general terms. It only means I'm ready to start
dating you."

There it was.

Out in the open.

The reality she had been trying so desperately to
avoid. He wanted more from her than friendship and she
was scared out of her ever-loving mind at the possibility.

The air in the vehicle suddenly seemed charged,
crackling with tension. She had to say something but had
no idea what.

"I... Chase—"

"Don't. Don't say it."

His voice was low, intense, with an edge to it she
rarely heard. She had so hoped they could return to the
easy friendship they had always known. Was that gone
forever, replaced by this jagged uneasiness?

"Say…what?"

"Whatever the hell you were gearing up for in that tone of voice like you were knocking on the door to tell me you just ran over my favorite dog."

"What do you want me to say?" she whispered.

"I sure as hell don't want you trying to set me up with another woman when you're the only one I want."

She stared at him, the heat in his voice rippling down her spine. She swallowed hard, not knowing what to say as awareness seemed to spread out to her fingertips, her shoulder blades, the muscles of her thighs.

He was so gorgeous and she couldn't help wondering what it would be like to taste that mouth that was only a few feet away.

She swallowed hard, not knowing what to say. He gazed down at her for a long, charged moment, then with a muffled curse, he leaned forward on the bench seat and lowered his mouth to hers.

Given the heat of his voice and the hunger she thought she glimpsed in his eyes, she might have expected the kiss to be intense, fierce.

She might have been able to resist that.

Instead, it was much, much worse.

It was soft and unbearably sweet, with a tenderness that completely overwhelmed her. His mouth tasted of caramel and apples and the wine he'd had at dinner—delectable and enticing—and she was astonished by the urge she had to throw her arms around him and never let go.

Don't miss
THE HOLIDAY GIFT by RaeAnne Thayne,
available December 2016 wherever
Harlequin® Special Edition books and ebooks are sold.

www.Harlequin.com

THE WORLD IS BETTER WITH

Romance

Harlequin has everything from contemporary, passionate and heartwarming to suspenseful and inspirational stories.

Whatever your mood, we have romance when you need it, wherever you are!

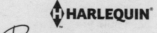

◆ HARLEQUIN®

A *Romance* FOR EVERY MOOD™

www.Harlequin.com

#RomanceWhenYouNeedIt

HSHMYBPA2016